The Treasure in the Royal Tower

The three girls stepped through the door and onto a small, square landing. "Now we're much closer to that thudding sound," George remarked softly.

"Shhh!" Nancy pointed to a closed door straight ahead of them. Light streamed through the thin crack around its edges.

"Somebody's in there," Bess whispered. "And that's definitely where the noises are coming from!"

Nancy nodded and moved quietly toward the door with George and Bess close behind. Nancy put her hand on the ornate brass doorknob and gave it a gentle turn. The door swung slowly open.

Through the door the girls saw a dazzling round room, its walls covered with brilliant embossed gold. But their eyes flew immediately to the far side of the room. All three gasped in surprise.

A man crouched close to the wall, glaring at them, a hammer clutched menacingly in one hand. . . .

Nancy Drew
Mystery Stories

Available from MINSTREL Books

NANCY DREW®

THE TREASURE IN THE ROYAL TOWER

CAROLYN KEENE

A
MINSTREL®
BOOK

PUBLISHED BY POCKET BOOKS

New York   London   Toronto   Sydney   Tokyo   Singapore

This book is a work of fiction. Names, characters, places and incidents are products of the author's imagination or are used fictitiously. Any resemblance to actual events or locales or persons, living or dead, is entirely coincidental.

A MINSTREL PAPERBACK *Original*

A Minstrel Book published by
POCKET BOOKS, a division of Simon & Schuster Inc.
1230 Avenue of the Americas, New York, NY 10020

Copyright © 1995 by Simon & Schuster Inc.

Produced by Mega-Books, Inc.

ISBN: 0-671-50502-5

First Minstrel Books printing December 1995

10 9 8 7 6 5 4 3 2 1

NANCY DREW, NANCY DREW MYSTERY STORIES, A MINSTREL BOOK and colophon are registered trademarks of Simon & Schuster Inc.

Cover art by Aleta Jenks

Printed in the U.S.A.

Contents

1

Trapped!

Nancy Drew peered through the windshield of her blue Mustang. "Hey, guys, this snow is something else," she said. "I can hardly see the road."

"Thank goodness we don't have much farther to go," George Fayne said as she reached over and turned up the defroster.

In the backseat, George's cousin Bess Marvin stretched and yawned. "Are we there yet?" she asked.

"Not quite," Nancy said as she gently tapped the brakes. "But maybe in another—"

"Look, Nancy, there's the sign," George interrupted, pointing out the blurry car window. " 'Butter Ridge Winter Sports Area—One Mile.' "

"Great," Nancy said. "Now, if we can just make it up this hill." She shifted the car to a

1

lower gear and skillfully guided the Mustang up the winding, unplowed road.

"Hey, cool!" Bess said, leaning forward excitedly. "Look at that huge building up ahead! It's like an old European palace."

"That must be Wickford Castle," Nancy said, "where we're staying—it's the ski resort's lodge. Keep your eyes open for the entrance."

She soon found a plowed drive leading from the main road up to a pair of iron gates. A stone pillar on the left held an intercom. Nancy rolled down the window, reached out, and pressed the button. A male voice answered, "Yes?"

"This is Nancy Drew, George Fayne, and Bess Marvin," Nancy replied. "We have reservations starting tonight."

"Sure thing," the voice replied. The gate automatically swung open, and the girls drove in.

The driveway curved around a stand of pine trees, and the castle loomed before them. Built of light-colored stone, it had four huge towers, one on each corner. The entrance was a massive arched wooden door, with three wide stone steps in front.

"Ooh, it's so creepy and romantic," Bess said as Nancy turned into a parking lot just past the steps. "I'll bet it won't take Nancy long to find a mystery to solve here."

"No way," Nancy said, pulling the Mustang into an empty spot. "This vacation is strictly for play."

"Sure, Nancy," Bess said, suppressing a giggle. "I think I've heard that one before."

Although she was only eighteen, Nancy Drew was an old hand at solving mysteries. She had even helped the police back home in River Heights crack some tough cases. Bess and George had learned from experience that wherever Nancy went, mysteries had a way of happening.

"This time I really mean it," Nancy said. Getting out of the car, she tucked her reddish blond shoulder-length hair up under her ski cap. "All I'm going to do this week is ski, skate, and have fun."

"I'm looking forward to our ski lessons with the champion skier from France," George put in, standing and stretching. "He sounds really good."

"And cute, too," Bess added as she got out. "At least judging by his picture in the brochure."

"Trust you to notice that," George teased.

Even though Bess and George were cousins and best friends, they were not at all alike. For blond, blue-eyed Bess, a good time might be an afternoon at the mall topped off by a visit to an ice cream shop. Slim, dark-haired George, in contrast, would choose a cross-country ski trip or a rugged hike.

"Hmm," Nancy said curiously, staring up at the castle. "Look at those four towers. I wonder why they don't match. The three closest to us are

3

all square and made of gray stone. But the one at the far end is round."

"Hey, you're right," George said. "And the stone is lighter, too—more like a cream color."

"Maybe the round tower is a later addition," Bess suggested. "And maybe the builders couldn't find the same kind of stone again. I'm sure it's no big deal. Can we get a move on? I'm freezing!"

Laughing, the girls gathered their bags and skis and headed for the castle's front door.

As they approached the steps, the door swung open. A tall, friendly young man wearing khakis and a red crewneck sweater stepped out. "Welcome to Wickford Castle," he said cheerfully. He took skis and poles from each of the girls. "You didn't need to carry all this stuff yourselves. We could have sent someone to help you."

"We don't mind," Nancy said. She stepped past him into a large reception hall. Craning her neck backward, she took in the soaring stone walls, vaulted ceiling, and huge brass chandelier. A grand staircase of carved stone, carpeted in dark blue, swept into the center of the lobby.

"You must be Nancy Drew and company from River Heights," the man said. "I'm Mark Lane, the owner of Butter Ridge. I hope you had a good drive up. Welcome to Wisconsin."

"We're sure glad to be here," Bess said, rubbing her hands together.

Mark propped the girls' skis against a nearby

4

rack. "We'll leave your skis here. They'll be taken to your lockers on the lower level. My wife, Christi, will assign you each a locker number and give you the combinations." He nodded toward a slender young woman with a long blond ponytail, grinning at them from the grand reception desk made of carved mahogany.

"You have a beautiful place here," George remarked.

"Thank you," Christi said, clearly pleased with the compliment. "We've worked hard on renovating Wickford Castle. It had been abandoned for a long time. When we bought it a couple of years ago, it was in pretty bad shape. Even now, not all of the wings are finished, but we're doing what we can."

"Well, it looks fantastic," George said, moving over to sign the register.

"And who is this?" Nancy asked as a large tan-and-white sheepdog ambled over to them.

"Oh, that's Gus," Christi said. "He's almost eight years old, but he thinks he's still a pup." She leaned over the desk and looked fondly down at the dog. "Don't you, boy?"

Gus wagged his tail and dropped contentedly on the floor next to Nancy. "Oh, he's found a friend," Mark said as Nancy bent down to pet the dog. "When Gus lies down at your feet that way, you know he's decided to attach himself to you."

"Well, that's fine with me," Nancy said with a smile as she gently rubbed behind the dog's ears.

"Oh, Dexter?" Christi called out.

Nancy turned to see a short, stout, gray-haired man carrying an armful of firewood from a back hallway. He wore overalls and a worn flannel shirt, as if he were a handyman. "This is Dexter Egan," Mark said. "He's been head caretaker at Wickford Castle for years."

"Afternoon," Dexter said briskly, keeping his head half-ducked. Nancy noted that his glance seemed to dart nervously around the lobby. Maybe he's not used to dealing with hotel guests, she told herself.

"Will you please help Ms. Drew and her friends with their luggage?" Mark asked Dexter.

With a nod, the caretaker dumped the firewood in a brass rack, then sidled over to pick up the girls' luggage.

"You're in room 304," Christi told the girls, handing them keys. "Dexter can take your bags now, but maybe you'd like to warm up by the fire before you go up." She gestured toward a large cozy lounge, just through a stone arch. A fire crackled in a huge fieldstone fireplace at the far end.

The girls headed gratefully for the fire. Nearby, on a leather sofa, a young woman sat curled up, reading a magazine. On a matching sofa across the room, two young couples laughed and joked. Sitting in an armchair by the fire was an older man with thick white hair, poring over a book. "The lodge seems to be busy," Nancy said to Mark.

He shrugged. "It'll take us a while to get established, but we've been lucky so far," he said. "Lisa," he called to the young woman on the couch. "I'd like you to meet our new guests. Nancy, Bess, George, this is Lisa Ostrum."

Lisa looked up and gave a friendly smile. Dressed in black stretch pants with a burgundy fleece pullover, Lisa was a tall, athletic-looking young woman with short brown hair.

"Lisa is a fantastic skier," Mark said, "and a writer for *Ski World* magazine. She did a great article about Butter Ridge in the fall issue. We're really pleased to have her here on a return visit."

Lisa grinned. "You guys are sure to love the slopes here," she said.

"Maybe you can give us some pointers," George said. "Working for *Ski World*, you must know a lot."

Lisa made a face. "I love skiing, but I'm afraid I'm no champion," she admitted. "Not like Mark's new ski teacher, Jacques."

Bess's eyes lit up. "We're supposed to be taking lessons with him," she said eagerly.

"Over there by the fireplace," Mark went on, "is Professor Hotchkiss. He's come all the way from Massachusetts. Those couples are Ken and Laura Hill and Jon and Chelsea Morton, all from Milwaukee. You'll meet them at dinner, tonight at seven. We like for all our guests to get to know one another."

Mark gave them directions on how to find their room, then left. After a few more minutes by the fire, the girls headed back through the lobby and up the big sweeping staircase.

Two flights up, the girls turned off down a wide wood-paneled hall. Gleaming wooden doors, each bearing a brass number plate, lined both sides of the corridor. At one point they passed a narrow, unlit hallway stretching off to the left. "Wow, this place goes on forever!" George exclaimed.

Room 304 was a few yards farther on. Nancy unlocked the door, and the girls walked in.

The room was large, with three casement windows. Its decor was homey, with rough plaster walls, comfortable-looking upholstered chairs, and thick patchwork quilts on the two queen-size beds.

Bess ran to a window. "Look, even though it's snowing, you can see the ski slopes," she said. "And the ice skating rink."

George joined her. "Too bad it's too late to hit the slopes today," she said.

"Dexter got all our luggage up here all right," Nancy reported, checking the pile of bags set beside the closet. "While you guys are gawking, I'm going to get unpacked."

A few minutes later, kneeling beside her bags, Nancy frowned. "What a bummer!" she said.

8

"My ski goggles are in my bootbag, and I need to treat them overnight with this antifog spray."

"I'll bet someone has taken them down to the basement lockers by now," George said.

"Probably," Nancy said. "I'll go down to the lower level and get them. You guys want to come?"

"Not me," Bess said. "I'm taking a hot bath."

"I'll come with you, Nancy," George said.

The two girls went back down the hall toward the main staircase. "Hey, look, Nan," George said, pausing as they passed a half-open door. "Here's some other stairs. If they go all the way to the lower level, this should save some time."

"It's worth trying," Nancy said. "This place is so big, any shortcut will help."

They started down the narrow, dimly lit wooden stairs. Three flights later, they came out into a large, brightly lit room with a linoleum floor. "This must be the place," George said.

Tall, black metal lockers lined the walls, with rows of low benches beside them, where skiers could sit to put on their boots. Off to one side was a closed wooden door with the words Ski School Office printed across it.

"My locker number's 73," Nancy said, pulling from her purse the slip of paper Christi had given her. They headed across the room, checking locker numbers. Nancy found her locker, dialed the combination, then opened the door to take out her goggles.

9

"Wonder what's down there?" George said, peering down a dark, dusty-looking concrete corridor opening off the locker room. After a few yards, the corridor made an abrupt right turn.

"Maybe that leads to a wing that Mark and Christi haven't renovated yet," Nancy said. Curious, she walked several feet down the corridor to see where it led. George followed.

Nancy halted suddenly, grabbing George's arm. "I thought I heard footsteps," Nancy said softly.

"You've been a detective too long, Nancy," George said with a chuckle. "You hear suspicious sounds everywhere you go."

"Okay, maybe it's nothing," Nancy said. "But it won't hurt to check it out."

The two girls continued on around the curving hallway, looking for a light switch to turn on. "Hey, look, George," Nancy murmured. "What do you suppose that is, up there?" She pointed to a large metal box mounted on the wall.

George stood on tiptoe and inspected the box. "It looks like some sort of power box, Nancy," she said. "It says Elevator on the front."

Nancy reached up and pushed open the tiny door on the front of the box. Inside was a single switch, set to the on position. "Where is the elevator this belongs to?" Nancy wondered. George shrugged.

They cautiously walked a few more yards,

around the next turn in the dark, doorless hallway. There, set into one wall, was a narrow wooden door with a small round window in it. "That must be it," Nancy declared.

She grabbed the brass handle and swung the door open. Behind it was an accordion-style inner door. When she slid that open, a dim overhead light switched on inside a tiny elevator cage.

Nancy peered inside. On one wall was a metal control panel with a row of buttons.

"What do you suppose this elevator is for?" George asked, stepping in behind Nancy.

"It may have been a service elevator, put in to help servants transport laundry," Nancy guessed. "But now I suspect it's used by skiers, going back and forth to their rooms."

"It sure beats climbing back up those stairs," George said. She curiously touched a small piece of mesh dangling from a ceiling hatch. "Should we give it a try?"

Nancy nodded. "Might as well."

She pulled the outer door shut, slid the accordion door closed, and pressed the button for the third floor. A motor began to hum. A second later the tiny elevator started to move upward.

Through the accordion door, they could see the bare walls of the elevator shaft. They passed a door labeled 1, then one labeled 2. "We're almost there," George said.

But as they neared the third floor, the elevator vibrated slightly. Nancy and George traded worried looks.

Then the tiny light in the ceiling began to flicker. The elevator slowed and gave another shake. The light flickered wildly.

"What's happening?" George asked.

"I don't know, but you'd better hang on," Nancy said.

The girls braced themselves against the sides of the tiny cage.

The elevator gave a noisy, violent shudder and stopped. Above them, the light flickered once more and then went out, plunging the tiny cage into darkness.

The girls were stuck between floors!

2

A Night of Surprises

Quickly Nancy slipped her penlight out of her purse and flashed it over the control panel. "Good," she said. "An emergency button."

She gave the button a push, but there was no response. She pushed it again harder and waited. Still no response.

"Great," she said with a sigh. "Apparently the emergency button doesn't work. Well, we'll just have to figure some way out of here." She ran the penlight's beam over the ceiling.

"Hey," George said, looking upward, "do you think we could make it up through that hatch?"

"You read my thoughts, George," Nancy said. "If we could get that mesh off, we probably could squeeze through. The elevator can't be too far from the third floor. If we go up through the hatch, then maybe we could reach the third-floor landing. At least we could bang on the door there and get someone's attention."

"Let's do it," George agreed. She reached up and gave the loose mesh a tug. It came off in her hands.

"Terrific," Nancy said, stuffing her penlight in her jeans pocket. She stood on tiptoe and gripped the frame of the hatch on two sides. "Good thing this ceiling isn't too high," she said.

"Here, I'll give you a boost." George bent down and wrapped her arms around Nancy's legs. As George lifted her up, Nancy pulled her head and shoulders up through the narrow hatch.

"What do you see?" George asked.

Nancy scrambled onto the elevator roof. "Tons of dust," she answered, shining the penlight around. "But the good news is, we're near the third-floor landing." She stood up. "I can almost touch the doorknob. This door must open to the hallway."

She reached up, hoping to grab the brass knob high above her. But just as her fingertips brushed it, her right foot slipped on some grease, sending her reeling against the side of the shaft. Quickly she reached out for the dusty wall, struggling to regain her balance.

"Nan, are you okay?" George called up anxiously.

"Just lost my footing for a moment," Nancy replied. "I'm fine now."

14

Nancy tipped her head back and studied the shaft above her. Twin steel pulleys held the elevator in place, each pulley sliding up and over gears caked with old grease. Trying to shimmy up one of those greasy pulleys was out of the question.

Nancy took a deep breath and, bracing herself against the dusty wall, once again stood on tiptoe and reached up toward the doorknob. Finally, with the tip of her fingers, she managed to touch it. Straining, she turned it to the right and the door opened. "Got it, George!" she called with a sigh of relief.

She grabbed the doorsill and hoisted herself up through the door into an unlit, deserted hallway. "Now let's get you up," she called back down to George.

"I'm on my way," George called from below.

Nancy stretched out on the floor and flashed the penlight down on the elevator's top. A moment later, George emerged through the hatch, with Nancy's purse slung over her shoulder. She pulled herself to her feet. "Here, catch!" She tossed Nancy's purse up to her, then quickly hoisted herself up to the landing. "Am I ever glad to be out of there!"

"You and me both," Nancy agreed.

"So where are we, anyway?" George asked, looking around.

"Somewhere on the third floor," Nancy said. "Maybe we're in that hallway we passed earlier

15

on the way to our room. There's some light coming from that end," she added, pointing. "Let's go that way."

"What do you think went wrong with the elevator?" George asked Nancy as they walked down the corridor.

"I'm not sure," Nancy said. "It could have been just an accident. Or . . ."

"Or what?" George asked.

"Or maybe something more," she said grimly. "After all, I did think I heard footsteps in that winding hallway downstairs. I definitely want to go down later and take another look at that switchbox."

A moment later the girls emerged in the main hallway. Studying the nearby door numbers, they soon got their bearings and were headed for room 304. "And not a moment too soon," George said, glancing at her watch. "Dinner is in five minutes. And I'm starving!"

Dinner was served in the castle's dining room, a large, stately room with tall, arched windows running along one wall. A long dining table, covered with a white linen cloth and silver place settings, stretched the length of the room. Matching oak chairs stood at each place.

As the guests gathered, Christi Lane introduced the girls to Dr. Maria Alvarez, a heart surgeon from Chicago, and her teenage daughter. Meg Alvarez was a tall, lively girl with dark eyes and shoulder-length brown hair. She and George were soon deep in conversation about Meg's high-school ski racing team.

As Nancy and Bess chatted with Dr. Alvarez, white-haired Professor Hotchkiss joined them. And a moment later, Nancy saw Lisa Ostrum, the freelance writer, enter the room.

"The Mortons and the Hills decided to go into the village to eat," Christi called out. "We have other guests arriving tonight, but they won't be checking in until late. So Jacques Brunais is the only other person we're expecting. He won't mind if we start without him. Please, folks, feel free to sit anywhere at the table."

"Jacques is our new head ski instructor," Mark said as the guests seated themselves. "Our other instructors are all part-time, but Jacques is full-time and lives here at the castle."

"You and Christi live here, too, right?" Meg Alvarez asked him.

Christi smiled. "You bet. We need to be here twenty-four hours a day," she said. "We have a whole wing where some staff members live— Dexter and Jacques and six others."

"This place sure is big," Bess commented.

Nancy thought of her recent adventure in the back corridors but decided not to mention it to the group. What if someone had deliberately tampered with the elevator—and that person was sitting at the table right now?

Just then a breathtakingly handsome young man entered the dining room. He had thick light brown hair, keen gray eyes, and strong, well-cut features. His bright charcoal-and-red Norwegian sweater emphasized his broad shoulders.

Smiling apologetically, he took a seat directly across from Bess. Bess gave Nancy an excited nudge in the ribs.

Mark introduced the guests to Jacques Brunais. "Meg, Nancy, Bess, and George are all scheduled to take lessons from you, Jacques," Mark explained. Then he added, "Jacques is in charge of our new teen program. It's attracted a number of young folks from surrounding areas."

"I'm delighted to meet you all," the ski instructor said shyly but politely, with a marked French accent. "I look forward to having you girls in my class."

A waiter came out from the kitchen, bringing a platter of grilled chicken and bowls of roast carrots and potatoes. Dinner was served family style, with guests helping themselves as the serving dishes were passed around.

As everyone began eating, Professor Hotchkiss asked Mark to tell the group more about Wickford Castle. "It's a magnificent structure," the professor observed in a dignified, slightly haughty voice. "Today I wandered around for a bit and noted some unusual features about the castle. I'm curious as to why they're there."

"What kind of features?" Nancy asked, remembering the mismatched towers outside.

"The building seems to have some strange false fronts and facades," Professor Hotchkiss said. "There's a stairway that goes nowhere and one or two dark tunnel-like corridors that simply come to an abrupt end. That sort of thing. None of it seems to serve any sensible purpose at all."

Remembering the twisting corridor on the lower level, Nancy shot George a meaningful glance.

"That was Ezra Wickford's idea," Mark replied. "He's the one who had the original castle built, back in the early 1920s. He wanted a place that would look exactly like an old castle."

"How interesting," Dr. Alvarez observed.

"At first we thought it was just his eccentric whim," Mark said. "But since buying the place, we've learned that it wasn't uncommon back then. In the 1920s, wealthy people often tried to copy European palaces. Sometimes they would buy entire rooms or sections from a castle in Europe. They'd have these sections taken apart, imported over here, and reassembled in their own mansions."

"And that's what Ezra Wickford did?" Dr. Alvarez asked.

"Yes," Mark replied. "In fact, he planned to import several more rooms. Some of those false fronts, Professor Hotchkiss, were built to lead to rooms that he never managed to buy. But other

19

ones were designed to conceal the imported rooms."

"I don't understand," Lisa Ostrum said with a puzzled frown.

Mark paused to help himself to the roast vegetables. "Apparently, Mr. Wickford was terrified of robbery," he said. "His mansion in Chicago had been burglarized a couple of times. So he built these dead-end passages to confuse intruders and hide the locations of the imported rooms."

"That's weird," Lisa murmured.

"How many imported rooms are there?" George asked.

"Well, he imported the library from an English manor," Mark said. "I can show that to you after dinner if you're interested. And he imported an entire tower from a chateau near the French Alps."

"That must be the tower on the north end," Nancy said, remembering the round tower. "So that's why it doesn't match the others."

Mark nodded. "Exactly," he said. "In fact, there's an intriguing story about that tower."

"Can you tell us?" Bess asked.

"According to local legend," Mark continued, "the queen of France, Marie Antoinette, used to visit that chateau during the French Revolution. Supposedly she used the tower as her own private wing."

"Fascinating," Professor Hotchkiss said, leaning forward with excitement. "French history is my specialty, you see. And Marie Antoinette is a particular favorite of mine."

"Well," Mark said, eyes twinkling, "then you would find our tower room of interest, because the people in the town near the chateau believed that Marie Antoinette hid something of value in that room. She was executed before she could come back to retrieve it. Whatever it was, it was never found."

"Neat!" Meg Alvarez said. "Can we see this room?"

"Unfortunately, no," Mark replied apologetically. "The round tower, or the Queen's Tower as we call it, has been sealed off for years. Eventually we hope to open it up and see what's there. But right now we have too many other expenses."

"But there are other things here in the castle from the same French chateau," Christi said. "Such as the mantel over the fireplace right here." Everyone turned to look at the dining room's grand fireplace. "That marble is hand-carved," Christi said. "And there's a whole set of rare French books up in the library. Mark, we'll have to give them a tour after dinner."

"Sounds great," Nancy said.

"I agree," Dr. Alvarez added.

"Right after dinner then," Mark said happily.

"And now the prize," Mark said, leading the guests on the tour down a ground-floor hall with

21

a high arched ceiling. "The library. It's an extraordinary room, with more than two thousand books, all from the chateau in France. Some of these books are very old indeed."

"And all in French, too, I bet," Lisa Ostrum joked. "Just my luck—I only took Spanish in high school."

"But the room itself is magnificent, too," Mark said as he opened the door. "It comes from an eighteenth-century English country house. Just take a look at the carved paneling."

Mark reached over to switch on the lights. As light flooded the room, Mark froze, with a gasp of horror. "What on earth? Oh, no!" he sputtered.

Nancy, Bess, and George, directly behind Mark, were the first to see what had shocked him so. The other guests clustered around, peering past him and the girls into the room.

Books lay in heaps everywhere. In one corner, a small bookcase was toppled sideways against the wall, books spilling every which way. Next to the fireplace a chunk of paneling had been gouged from the wall and thrown onto the floor. A large oil painting in an ornate gilt frame teetered upside down against a brocade armchair.

The library had been vandalized!

3

Noises in the Night

Looking over Mark's shoulder, Christi cried out in shock, "Why would anyone do a thing like this?"

"I can't imagine," Mark said numbly as they gazed around the ransacked library.

Nancy stepped back, away from the room. "Maybe the best thing would be for all of us to leave," she said. "If we touch things, we could destroy an important clue."

"Good suggestion," Mark said, pulling a ring of keys out of his pocket. "I should just lock the place up. We'll get the police here in the morning."

Mark and Christi backed out of the library. Mark closed the door, locking it securely.

Dazed, the guests shuffled back down the hallway to the lounge. Some stayed there to chat, while others went up to their rooms.

Glancing around, Nancy motioned to her friends. "Something really strange is going on around here," she said to them quietly. "First, our little mishap with the elevator. And now this."

"Maybe we should volunteer to help Mark and Christi," George said. "If only they knew they had a trained detective here under their roof . . ."

Nancy needed no urging. She spun around and headed for the front desk, George and Bess right behind her. "Mark, Christi," Nancy said as the girls approached him at the desk, "could we see you for a moment?"

"Of course, Nancy," Mark said, looking up wearily. "Let's go to the office, where we can sit down." He and Christi led the girls behind the desk into a carpeted back hallway, stopping at a door that stood slightly ajar. "Here we are," he said, pushing the door open and gesturing for the girls to walk in.

The office was a small, cozy room. A kneehole desk faced the door, with three comfortable-looking chairs grouped next to it. A large picture window overlooked the ski slopes, brilliant white under floodlights at night.

Gus, the sheepdog, rose from the corner where he had been sleeping. He padded across the room to reach Nancy's side. Grinning, she reached down and petted his head.

"We'd really like to help you find out what's

24

happened to your library," Nancy began. "George, Bess, and I have some experience in detective work."

"There's never been a mystery in River Heights that Nancy couldn't solve," Bess added loyally.

"We'd be grateful for anything that you can do," Mark said, looking somewhat surprised.

"To begin with then," Nancy said, "when do you think the vandalism happened? When was the last time either of you were in the library?"

"I haven't been in there for three or four days," Christi admitted.

"I was there yesterday, right after lunch," Mark said. "On Saturday. Everything was fine then."

"So the vandalism happened either yesterday afternoon or evening or earlier today," Nancy said. "What about the guests—when did they check in?"

"Saturday is the most popular day for starting a ski week," Christi said. "Except for you guys, they all checked in yesterday, between noon and midnight." She counted them off on her fingers. "Eight guests—the Mortons, the Hills, Dr. Alvarez and Meg, Lisa Ostrum, and the professor. The times of arrival will be on the check-in list. Five other guests all left Saturday morning before lunch."

"So eight guests were here when the vandalism

occurred," Nancy said. "Who else might have been in the castle?"

"On a weekend, there wouldn't have been anyone here for repairs or deliveries," Mark said.

"The castle is surrounded by an iron fence," Christi explained. "The only way to get in is through the gate, which we monitor with video cameras. A shuttle bus from the village brings local people for sports, but they go to the ski hut or the skating rink or the snowmobile stand—never into the castle."

"What about the staff?" Nancy asked.

"Only the housekeeper goes into the library," Christi said, "and she cleans it on Wednesday. No other staff member has any reason to go in there."

"But they still have access," Nancy pointed out. "It would be a good idea for you to question all the staff members—learn their whereabouts from Saturday noon on. I'd question them myself, but it's best if no one knows yet that I'm a detective."

Mark and Christi exchanged worried glances. "There's something else you should know, Nancy," Mark added quietly. "This isn't our first incident."

"You mean there have been other problems at Wickford Castle?" Nancy asked. "Like what?"

"Peculiar things happening at night," Mark said. "Odd noises mainly."

"And we can't figure out where these noises are coming from," Christi added.

"What kind of noises?" Nancy asked.

"Thudding sounds," Mark replied. "They seem to come from somewhere above us. I've searched the attic several times, but I just can't find any explanation. And if guests start hearing them—"

"It could put Wickford Castle right out of business," Christi finished his sentence.

Nancy was quiet for a moment as she watched the young couple. They seemed genuinely upset, she thought. Her instincts told her that they were innocent of whatever was happening. "I hope that it's not long before we get to the bottom of things," she said, standing up.

"We'll do everything we can," George added.

"Great," Mark said.

"Oh, one other thing, Mark," Nancy said. "About the back elevator. Is it ever turned off?"

"Not that I know of," Mark said, looking surprised. "It isn't used much. Once in a while some skiers find it and go up in it. Why do you ask?"

"George and I used it this afternoon," she explained. "It stopped before it got all the way to our floor." She threw a glance at George, silently warning her to downplay the incident.

"It probably needs a checkup," Christi said. "I'll see to it. Anyway, thanks for your help,

27

Nancy. Let us know if you need any information."

"Sounds good," Nancy said. After saying good night, the girls left and headed back to the lobby.

"Hey, Nancy," George said, "do you still want to go back down to the basement to check that elevator switchbox?"

"Definitely, George," Nancy said.

In the lobby the girls found a wide flight of steps leading down to the locker room. They strolled down, trying to look as casual as possible. After crossing the brightly lit locker room, they entered the dark back hallway and turned the corner to find the switchbox.

Shining her penlight on the metal box, Nancy opened its small door and flashed the light inside. "Look at this!" she said as the others peered over her shoulder. "The switch says Off now. But when we got on the elevator this afternoon, George, that switch was set here, next to the arrow that says On."

"Somebody must have come along and turned the elevator power off," George said. "And it must have been while we were on our way to the third floor. Do you think it was the same person whose footsteps you heard, Nancy?"

"Possibly," Nancy said.

"But why would anyone turn the power off on you guys?" Bess asked.

"To scare us maybe," Nancy said. "Someone may be afraid we'll find out something—

28

something they'd rather keep secret. Well, let's check to see if it's working okay now."

Nancy flipped the power switch back to On. Then the girls went around the corner and pushed the wall button to summon the elevator. Up above the elevator made some low grumbling sounds, then slowly came back down the shaft.

"It's working fine now," George said, pushing open the door. "Even the light is on."

"I still think I'd rather not ride back up in that thing," Bess said with a shudder.

"I'll pass, too, Bess," George said. "Getting stuck once was enough for me." She shut the door and they headed back toward the locker room.

Returning upstairs, the girls wandered to the lounge to see if any guests were still hanging around. They found no one but Meg Alvarez, huddled forlornly in an armchair in front of the TV set. "Hey, Meg," George said. "What's up?"

"Just getting up my nerve to go upstairs alone," Meg explained. "My mom turned in an hour ago." She reached for the remote control and snapped off the TV. "Mind if I walk up with you guys?"

"Of course not," Nancy said. "But why would you be nervous about going upstairs alone?"

"Partly it was seeing that library tonight," Meg said as she rose to her feet. "Somebody sure did a number on it."

"You can say that again," George agreed.

"But I also got spooked by a lot of noise out in the hall last night," Meg added as they walked toward the main stairs.

"What kind of noise?" Nancy asked alertly.

"It was a couple of men talking real loud," Meg replied. "I got up and peeked out to see who it was. I'm pretty sure one of them was Jacques—you know, the ski instructor."

"The cute one," Bess put in.

"He sure is," Meg agreed, her eyes sparkling. "I'm not positive who the other man was, but I think it was the caretaker."

"You mean Dexter Egan?" George asked.

"Right. He gives me the creeps," Meg confessed. "I don't like the way he slinks around and won't look you in the eye."

"Oh, I think he's just shy," Bess said sympathetically.

"Could you tell what they were arguing about?" Nancy asked as they reached the second floor.

"No, sorry. I couldn't," Meg said. "Well, this is where I turn off—our room is just a couple doors down this hall."

"Hi, everyone. What's going on?"

The girls turned in surprise. Lisa Ostrum was coming down the hall, wearing a flannel sleep-shirt and a colorful snowflake-patterned robe. In one hand, she carried a large towel.

"We were just talking about all the spooky stuff that's going on here," Bess said.

"Yeah, isn't it something!" Lisa said, laughing as she rubbed her wet hair with the towel. "Secret rooms, hidden treasures, and now a mysterious vandal in the library. Next they'll be asking us to believe that this castle is haunted."

"But you saw how the library was messed up," Meg said, her voice quavering. "Someone really did that."

"Probably someone on the staff who didn't get a big enough raise," Lisa said skeptically. "Well, good night. See you on the slopes tomorrow."

"See you," Meg echoed. She followed Lisa down the second-floor hallway, while Nancy and the cousins climbed on up the stairs to their floor.

In the middle of the night, Nancy woke up with a start. Somewhere in the distance, she could hear a strange, steady thumping noise.

In the bed she shared with Bess, George stirred and then propped herself up on one elbow. "What's that?" she asked groggily.

"I'm not sure," Nancy said, sitting up. "But I wonder if it's the same noises Mark and Christi told us about." She slid out of bed and grabbed her jeans from a nearby chair. "Let's check it out."

They quickly roused Bess from her side of the bed. All three girls pulled on some clothes, Nancy got her penlight, and they stepped cautiously into the hall. Small lighting fixtures mounted on the walls provided a soft, low light.

"I can still hear that thumping," George said quietly. "It sounds like it's coming from this way." She pointed away from the main stairs. The girls quietly began to walk in that direction.

A few doors down, the hallway ended, with another corridor going off to the left. Nancy tried to picture how the lodge's floor plan fit into the exterior layout. "This could be heading toward the round tower," Nancy whispered.

"The one Mark called the Queen's Tower?" Bess asked.

"Yes," Nancy said. "At any rate, this is where the thudding sounds are coming from. Come on, let's see where the hallway goes."

The girls crept down the narrow hall. Eerie colored moonlight filtered through stained-glass windows along one wall. But on the other wall, there were no doors or arches leading to any rooms.

"I think we're getting closer," Nancy said, snapping on her penlight. The girls stopped and listened. The sounds were louder now.

"It's like someone hammering," George said.

"But look ahead—the hallway ends right there," Bess said, pointing forward. Nancy flashed her light in that direction. "And there's nothing there—no doors, no stairs—it just ends. This must be one of those hallways to nowhere that the professor was talking about."

"Listen," George whispered, clutching Nancy's elbow. "The thudding noises have stopped."

"But now I hear something else," Bess said. "Right on the other side of that end wall."

Nancy hurried over to the end wall and put her ear against it. She listened intently. "Footsteps," she reported in a hushed voice.

George and Bess pressed their ears against the wall, too. "They're really loud," Bess whispered.

"And they echo," Nancy said softly. "As though they're coming from inside some huge empty space." She listened some more. "It sounds like they're circling around," she said. "As if someone was going down a spiral staircase."

Bess's eyes grew wide. "Like—inside a round tower?" she guessed.

"But Mark said the round tower is sealed off," George said. "How could someone be inside it?"

"I don't know," Nancy said. "But *somebody's* on the other side of this wall. And whoever it is definitely has got something to hide!"

4

A Day of Adventure

The girls stood frozen still, ears pressed against the wall as they listened to the mysterious footsteps become louder and louder.

Then gradually the steps began to fade into the distance. The three girls drew deep breaths.

"Let me check something," Nancy said softly. She faced the end wall and gave it a firm tap with her penlight. Then she went to the side wall with the stained-glass windows and did the same.

"Just as I suspected," she said. "The end wall has an entirely different sound. Hear the difference?" She tapped each of the two walls again.

"Compared to the wall with the windows," George said, "the end wall has a hollow sound."

"Right," Nancy agreed. "The side wall is an exterior wall—it separates us from the outside. Exterior walls are heavier and have a thick, duller sound. But walls that separate inside rooms are thinner and have a more hollow sound."

"So there's a room on the other side of this wall," Bess said. "Like the Queen's Tower?"

"I think you're right, Bess," Nancy said.

With no place else to go, the girls started back down the corridor. "But I don't get it," George said. "Even if the Queen's Tower is on the other side of that wall, how could anyone be walking around in there? Mark said it was sealed off."

"Maybe someone found a way in, one that Mark doesn't know about," Bess pointed out.

"Could be," Nancy said. "Tomorrow, let's ask Mark for the castle's floor plans. Then we'll look for an entrance to the tower—a hidden entrance."

Monday morning after breakfast, the three girls met Meg Alvarez by the lockers to wait for Jacques Brunais. Nancy had warned Bess and George not to mention the noises they'd heard last night. There were plenty of other things to talk about, though. "I can't believe how gorgeous Jacques is," Bess was saying with an exaggerated sigh.

"To die for," Meg agreed. "You know who he reminds me of? Do you watch that soap opera on—"

Just then the ski school office door opened. Jacques stepped out, wearing a sleek, bright purple one-piece ski suit and a matching stocking cap with a long tassel. "Ready for your lesson, ladies?" he said with a smile. The girls nodded and gathered around.

"First, we'll go to the top of the mountain," Jacques explained. "There I will watch each of you ski and get an idea of your skill levels. So let's go outside, get our skis on, and head for the lift."

Outside, the girls quickly put on their skis and tramped over to the triple chair lift. Each girl waited her turn to get on. Nancy, George, and Meg shared one of the three-seat hanging chairs, suspended from an overhead cable. As the cable moved, the chair glided through the air toward the top of the small mountain.

Beneath them the ski slopes, white and fresh from yesterday's snow, were dazzling in the morning sun. "Hey, this snow is awesome," Meg said, looking down. "I can't wait to lay down those first tracks."

"I'm with you, Meg," Nancy said happily.

"Where's Bess?" George asked, twisting around in her seat to look behind her.

"Guess," Nancy said, giggling. "She's riding up on the lift with Jacques."

George groaned. "Why am I not surprised!"

"Well, the guy is totally cool," Meg said. "You've got to admire her taste."

Soon all four girls and Jacques met at the top of the mountain. The girls lined up on a short slope, and each made a run while Jacques watched.

When they had finished, he said, "Meg and George, you two should work on your racing skills. Nancy and Bess, you could use more time on your parallel turns." Jacques arranged to work with Meg and George first for an hour; then, after a cocoa break, he'd spend the final morning hour with Nancy and Bess.

Bess watched wistfully as Jacques swooshed off with George and Meg. "Hey, look at that trail," Nancy called out to distract her. "It goes around to the back of the mountain. Let's try it."

"Sounds good," Bess replied. A moment later, the girls were sailing down the mountain's back, winding in and out of tall, snow-covered pines. Shifting her weight from ski to ski, Nancy carved long graceful arcs through the fresh powder. Though it was her first time skiing that season, she soon felt herself relax into an easy, natural rhythm.

It didn't take long for Bess to get caught up in the fun either. She laughed happily as she snowplowed to a stop beside Nancy, who had just halted. "What's up?" Bess asked.

"Look down there, through the trees," Nancy said, pointing toward the bottom of the slope. "Isn't that Dexter Egan walking through the snow? He's heading toward that shed over there."

Bess nodded. "It sure looks like him," she said. "But I thought he worked inside the castle."

They watched as Dexter disappeared inside

37

the shed. "That looks like where the machinery that runs the back ski lift is kept," Nancy mused. "Oh, well, maybe he's doing some repairs. I guess it doesn't matter. Come on, Bess, I'll race you to the lift."

"You're on," Bess called. The two girls took off, picking up speed as they raced down the slope.

Trooping through the lobby after a full day's skiing, the girls were met by Gus, the sheepdog. His toenails clicked on the stone floor as he ran to nuzzle Nancy's hand. "That reminds me, guys," Nancy said. "I should find Mark and Christi and see what happened when the police checked out the library."

Bess, exhausted, slumped against a great carved post at the bottom of the main stairway. "I guess you want us to come with you," she said reluctantly.

George chuckled. "I'll come," she offered. "Anything to avoid climbing stairs with these sore muscles!"

The three girls went down the small hallway behind the desk and tapped on the office door. "Come in," they heard Christi call.

Christi was sitting alone at the desk as they entered. "Any news from the police?" Nancy asked.

Christi shook her head and sighed. "They didn't turn up any clues," she said. "And they

38

don't seem very concerned—unless we can prove it's a robbery. They asked me and Mark to check to see if anything was stolen, but we haven't had time yet. Frankly, we don't even have a list of all those books. Something could be missing and we'd never know."

"Did you have time to ask everyone on staff where they were Saturday and Sunday?" Nancy asked.

Christi nodded. "Everyone has an alibi," she reported. "They were either working or away from the castle. And they're all people I trust."

"Could we inspect the library?" Nancy asked. "We might be able to find a clue—something the police missed."

"Be my guest," Christi said, picking up a large key ring from the desk. She slipped off one key and handed it to Nancy.

"Oh, and one other thing," Nancy said as she took the key. "Last night we heard some of the noises you told us about. We may even have pinpointed where they're coming from. Any chance we could see floor plans of the castle?"

Christi bit her lip. "Sorry," she said. "The only plans we have are for areas we've renovated. You're welcome to those, of course." She scooted her chair over to a file cabinet, opened a drawer, and took out some big sheets of paper, all rolled up. "When we bought the castle," she added, "we asked for the original plans, but they had been either lost or destroyed. Your best bet for details is Dexter Egan. He knows the castle better than anyone."

Nancy's instincts perked up. "How long has he worked here?" she asked, taking the plans.

"Thirty years, he told us," Christi said. "Even when the castle was abandoned, he watched over it."

"He must be a handy guy to have on staff," Nancy commented, subtly digging for information. "What does he do around here?"

"Oh, he's a jack-of-all-trades," Christi said. "He does repairs on the castle and helps us when guests are arriving. Sometimes he drives the snowcat for the crew that grooms the slopes each morning. And he helps maintain the lift equipment. Why do you ask, Nancy?"

"Just curious," Nancy said. So that explained his presence out on the slopes today, she thought to herself as she stood up. "Thanks for the key."

"Thanks for your help," Christi replied, waving as the girls left the office.

"You're really suspicious of Dexter, aren't you, Nancy?" George asked out in the hall.

"I'm suspicious of everyone," Nancy said. "And Meg did say Dexter was arguing with Jacques in the hall the other night."

Bess stopped and looked at Nancy. "Don't tell me you suspect Jacques!" she protested.

"Yes, Bess, even Jacques," Nancy said firmly.

Nancy led the way back through the lobby and

40

on to the library. After unlocking the door, she snapped on the overhead light. "Wow, what a mess!"

"For sure," George said, walking to a nearby window and pulling back its heavy maroon drapes. A few rays of fading afternoon light filtered in.

"Look at all these," Bess said, kneeling beside a pile of musty-smelling books.

Nancy sat beside her and picked up a book. As she opened it, its pages crackled with age. "Look at this," she said. "There are fingerprints on the cover of this book. It looks as though someone has read it recently."

"This one, too" George said. "It's all dusty except for the fingerprints."

"This might mean that our vandal wasn't just messing things up for a grudge. He or she may have been looking for specific information in these books."

"Whoever it was must have a knack for languages," Bess said, flipping through some pages. "They're all written in French."

"Or maybe it was someone who speaks French," Nancy said. "Like Jacques."

"Lots of people speak French," Bess said, quickly rising to Jacques's defense. "I'll bet you can read these books, Nancy—you had three years of French at River Heights High."

"I'll try," Nancy said, picking up a small book with a bright red cover. She pored over a page for a minute. "Hey, this book is about Marie Antoi-nette. And it's real old—dated 1800."

"I wonder if it mentions the chateau that Mark said the tower came from," George said eagerly.

"It might," Nancy said, shutting the book and getting to her feet. "I'll take it back to the room and look at it later."

Just then Nancy tensed up, her senses alerted. She held up one hand, signaling the other girls.

"That snow was really great today," Nancy said, acting casual. Meanwhile, she groped in her pocket, found a pencil, and scribbled on the building plans Christi had given her: "Someone is in the room."

She showed the note to George and Bess. They looked up in surprise. "Uh, yeah, the skiing was fantastic," George said, trying to keep up the pretend conversation.

Nancy nodded toward the window at the far end of the library, where the maroon drapes were still closed. George and Bess followed her gaze. They all saw the heavy drapes sway slightly.

No doubt about it—someone was hiding there!

42

5

Strange Happenings

"And the trails here are so excellent," Nancy kept improvising to fool the eavesdropper. She motioned to the cousins to move toward the library door, to act as if they were leaving.

"We definitely have to come here again," George agreed as she snapped off the light. Then, in response to Nancy's signal, she opened and slowly shut the door into the hall to make the eavesdropper think they'd gone. The girls then ducked behind some nearby armchairs and waited.

Nancy peered through the twilight that fell through the partly opened drapes, straining to hear any sound. But everything in the library was still.

Then, from the far end of the room, she heard a soft rustling sound. A figure slipped out from

43

behind the drapes and paused for a second. The girls waited tensely, not daring to breathe.

A flashlight snapped on. The figure began to cross the room, running a beam of light wildly up and down the wall. Nancy strained to make out the person's face, but the small bright beam from the flashlight threw the figure behind it into shadow.

Suddenly the light hit the large gouge in the wall paneling and stopped there. The figure moved closer to the gouge and flashed the light inside it. He or she reached inside the opening, as though searching for something.

At last, the figure moved away from the wall. Still sweeping the flashlight along the floor, the person headed toward the door to the hall. Then the person hesitated and stopped, turning back to look at the library. Once again the flashlight beam ran slowly across the floor, along the walls—and then lingered on the armchairs that Nancy and the cousins were hiding behind.

The girls crouched, not moving.

Nancy's mind raced, considering strategy. Should she confront the person? she wondered. If she did, she would find out who it was and maybe why that person was in the library. But if she did that, she reminded herself, whoever it was would then know that she was investigating the case. And if this was the person who'd vandalized the library, he or she would be careful not to let Nancy learn any more information.

44

Revealing herself as a detective was not a wise idea, Nancy decided. It was too important that she keep her cover, at least for now.

The flashlight's beam roamed once more around the room and along the walls. Nancy sat quietly, scarcely breathing. She desperately hoped that the light would not settle on either the cousins or her.

Finally, the figure turned and opened the door. The glare from the hallway light hit the person's face. Nancy caught her breath.

It was Dexter Egan.

He stepped out into the hall and closed the door. Bess started to move, but Nancy touched her arm, signaling her to wait.

After a few moments, Nancy stood up and cautiously moved toward the hall door. She opened it and peered down the hall, searching in both directions.

"It's okay now," she said quietly, closing the door and snapping on the light. "He's gone."

"But what was he doing here?" George asked.

"It looked like he was searching for something," Nancy said. "The question is, what?"

She walked over to the large gouge in the wall, rose on her tiptoes, and peered in. "Let's see if there's anything in here," she said, reaching in and fumbling around.

The vandal had dug through the thick wood panel into the plaster wall behind it, making an opening roughly one foot long, four inches wide,

45

and seven inches deep. "No, there's nothing here but splintered wood and crumbling plaster," she said finally, pulling out her arm.

"But maybe Dexter thought there was something," Bess pointed out.

"Or he could already have found whatever was there and taken it with him," George added.

"Either way," Nancy said, "if Dexter was our vandal, why would he come back to look in the hole again? The vandal probably had plenty of time to look when he ransacked the library the first time."

"Unless he was surprised in the act then," George suggested.

Nancy sighed. "That's true," she admitted. "There are so many factors we don't know yet. Maybe we need to approach this from a different angle."

"What do you mean, Nan?" Bess asked.

"We keep asking ourselves *who* ransacked the library," Nancy explained. "Maybe it would help instead to ask ourselves *why*."

Glancing around, George's eyes lit on the large oil portrait lying upside down against a nearby armchair. It showed a gray-haired man in a black suit with a fierce expression on his face.

"I guess this picture originally hung over that spot where the gouge is," George said. "Maybe the vandal thought that there was a wall safe behind it—you know, a place to hide money or

46

jewels. Mark did say that old Ezra Wickford was paranoid about being robbed. It makes sense that he would have lots of hiding places built into the castle."

Nancy shook her head. "A wall safe would be a box built into the wall, with a door and a lock on it," she said. "There's nothing in that wall but rough plaster."

"If the vandal was looking for a wall safe," Bess said, looking around the room, "why did he or she mess up all the books, too? And why stop to read some of the books?"

Nancy shook her head, feeling baffled. "Listen, guys, I don't think we'll learn anything more here tonight," she said. "Let's head on back to our room. We could all use a hot shower, I'm sure."

Picking up the red book about Marie Antoinette, she led the way to the door. As the girls left the room, they snapped out the light and locked the door behind them.

When they returned to the office, Mark was there instead of Christi. "We were just looking for clues in the library," Nancy told him, laying the library key on his desk. "We didn't find much, I'm afraid. Do you mind if I borrow this for bedtime reading, though?" She held up the red book.

"Help yourself," Mark said. "We like our guests to read our books while they're here."

"You might as well straighten up the library so guests can use it again," Nancy told him. "There's no need to keep it off limits anymore."

"Great," Mark said, relieved. "Do you know yet why the room was vandalized?"

"Someone was definitely searching for something," Nancy said, "though I'm not exactly sure what. And I don't know whether the vandal found it or not."

Mark shook his head, clearly puzzled. "Do you have any idea who it was?" he asked.

"I can't prove who did the vandalism," Nancy said cautiously. She turned to make sure the office door was shut before she added, "But somebody was in there today, acting very suspiciously."

"Who?" Mark asked.

"Dexter Egan," Nancy said. "We must have surprised him when we came in. He hid behind the drapes. He doesn't know that we saw him. Does Dexter have a set of keys to every room in the castle?"

"Yes, he does," Mark said, sounding worried. "But he knew the library was supposed to be off limits. He's always been trustworthy. . . ."

"And he may still be," Nancy reassured Mark. "But even so, I'd like to get a bit more information about him. For example, Christi said that even when the castle was abandoned, Dexter stayed on here as caretaker. Do you know why or who was paying him during that time?"

48

"I assume the former owners were paying him," Mark replied. "That's just what he told us when we hired him."

"I see," Nancy said thoughtfully. "And what about his background? Where is he from?"

"He told us he'd lived all his life in the village of Butter Ridge," Mark said. "I have to admit, I really don't know much about him. He sort of came with the property—he was taking care of things when we bought the place, and we just kept him on. We never asked him for references. I'm glad you told me about finding him in the library. I'll have a little talk with him and see just what—"

"Wait a minute, Mark," Nancy interrupted. "It might be better if you didn't talk to Dexter about the library. We still have no proof he was the vandal. And I don't want word to get out that I'm investigating this case."

"Agreed," Mark said as the girls started toward the door. "I won't mention any of this to Dexter until I get the okay from you."

That night after dinner, Nancy sat cross-legged on her bed, poring over the red book. "I'll never figure this all out," she said. "My French is too rusty."

"How about asking Professor Hotchkiss?" George asked, looking up from the castle's plans. "He's an expert in French history. I'll bet he knows French."

"He probably does," Nancy said thoughtfully. "But you know, I'm not quite sure about him. I don't understand why he's here."

"He's here to ski," Bess replied. "Just like we are. I saw him out on the slopes today."

"Yes, but why here?" Nancy persisted. "He's from northern Massachusetts, near where they have some of the best ski slopes in the country. So why travel to Wisconsin for a ski vacation? It doesn't add up."

"Good point," Bess said.

Then Nancy suddenly sat up straight. "Hey, what's that sound?" she asked.

Bess and George fell silent immediately and turned their heads to listen.

A woman's voice rang through the outside hall, followed by a fierce, muffled banging. "Let me out!" the woman was calling frantically. "Please! Somebody help me!"

The loud banging echoed again down the hall. "Somebody!" she called. "Please help! I'm trapped!"

6

The Figure in Black

The girls jumped to their feet and hurried into the hallway outside their room. "This way," Nancy said, nodding toward the right. As they ran down the hall, the shouts for help became louder and louder.

Following the sound of the woman's cries, they turned down the small side hallway leading to the back elevator. Nancy found a light switch and snapped it on. "Behind that door on the left," Nancy called, pointing to a narrow door with a tarnished brass knob. "The shouts are coming from there."

She grabbed the doorknob and gave it a hard pull, but it wouldn't open.

"Somebody help me!" the woman shouted. "I'm locked in!" The door rattled wildly. "Somebody, please!"

"That sounds like Lisa!" Bess said.

51

"It sure does, Bess," Nancy said, giving the doorknob another tug. "Lisa? Is that you?"

"Yes!" Lisa called back. "Hey, Nancy, get me out of here, will you?"

"We're trying, Lisa," Nancy replied. "Hang on."

"What happened?" said a woman's voice behind them. "Can I help?"

"Oh, Dr. Alvarez," Nancy said, turning around to see the doctor striding down the hall toward them. "It's Lisa. She's locked in here."

"How'd she do that?" Meg Alvarez asked as she hurried up next to her mother.

Before Nancy could answer, Professor Hotchkiss also came around the corner from the main hallway. "What on earth is going on?" he asked. "I was in my room, and I heard all this commotion . . ."

Quickly George explained Lisa's predicament.

"But doesn't anyone have a duplicate key?" the professor asked.

"Yes, sir. I do, sir," a voice down the hall called out. Everyone turned to see Dexter Egan's short, stout figure trotting toward the door. A large ring of keys dangled from his belt. "Don't understand how this could have happened," he muttered as he fumbled for the right key. "How did the lady get locked in this way?"

He pulled a very large, rusty-looking key from the ring, slid it in the lock, and turned it.

Lisa burst through the opened door, dressed in

jeans and a pullover, her camera dangling around her neck. "Who locked me in there?" she demanded angrily.

"Wait a minute, Lisa," Bess said. "What makes you think somebody locked you in?"

"Of course somebody locked me in," Lisa said impatiently. "A key was sitting right there in the keyhole. I saw it. It was a large, old-looking key, almost like an antique. I turned the key and opened the door so I could check out those crazy stairs. I guess the door swung shut behind me. When I found out what the stairs were all about, I headed back down in a hurry. But by then the door was locked! I want to know who locked it— and why!"

Dexter cleared his throat. "The lady's right about that key," he said gruffly. "I saw it there myself this morning, just like it usually is."

"But why would anyone lock you in?" Professor Hotchkiss asked.

Lisa glared at him. "I don't know, Professor," she said. "Do you? You're the one who was talking at dinner last night about the stairs that led nowhere. You knew they were here."

Nancy held up her hand. "Wait a minute, everyone," she said. "Let's start at the beginning. Lisa, why were you checking out those stairs in the first place?"

Lisa sighed impatiently. "I'm writing a new article for *Ski World* and need a good photograph to go with it," she said. "I always do my own photography. I wanted a panoramic nighttime shot of the slopes, and I thought I could get a good angle from high up in the castle. I happened to open this door, which was unlocked, and I saw these stairs. I figured they led to another floor."

"That's logical," Dr. Alvarez commented.

"Yeah, well, those stairs are phony," Lisa said with disgust. "They go up about twenty steps to a landing, turn a corner, then they run into a wall. The stairs just stop. It's so stupid."

Professor Hotchkiss cleared his throat. "Those *are* the stairs I was talking about the other night," he said. "The day I arrived, I was wandering around the castle, and I, too, saw the key in this lock."

"Like I said, it's always kept there," Dexter Egan put in, scratching his grizzled head.

"I turned the key, opened the door, and started up the stairs," the professor continued. "I discovered just what Lisa has found. These stairs go nowhere."

"Old Mr. Wickford had 'em built that way," Dexter said with an odd chuckle.

At that moment Mark and Christi came running down the hall. "What happened?" Christi asked in a worried voice.

"Those dumb stairs," Lisa replied. "I got trapped in there."

"Oh, no," Christi said. "Wasn't the key in the lock outside?"

"Yes—and somebody turned it and locked me in," Lisa declared, giving her camera strap a frustrated tug. "If the stairs don't go anywhere, why don't you just board the dumb things up?"

Mark winced. "Board up the castle's eccentric features?" he said soothingly. "We've always thought that was one of the things that makes the castle a special place to stay."

"It's true, those are the touches that make this place charming," Dr. Alvarez said.

"Well, you try getting locked into a tiny dark place like that, and see how charming it is then!" Lisa fumed.

"You're right, Lisa," Christi said. "I don't know why we left that key in the lock. I guess it just never occurred to us that anybody would turn the key while someone else was up there."

Nancy traded glances with Bess and George. Christi had a point, Nancy was thinking—it was odd that anyone would turn the key on Lisa. Had it been an accident, or did someone mean to trap her? And where was the key now?

"We're just glad you're all right," Mark said to Lisa. "Please accept our apologies. Dexter, first thing tomorrow, remove the lock from this door. That way, this kind of incident will never happen again."

Lisa made a little huffing sound, but she seemed placated. Dr. Alvarez and Meg walked with her back to the second floor, while the other guests headed back to their rooms.

As the girls left, Nancy turned to see Dexter Egan kneel beside the door to study the lock. He looked up and saw her watching him. Nancy turned away and quickly walked on. But she couldn't shake the impression that he had given her a very nasty look.

"I think I'm going to quit early today," Nancy said the next afternoon as the girls skied to the bottom of the slopes. She peered up through the heavily falling snow. "With the snow coming down this hard, it's impossible to see the trail."

"I'm with you, Nancy," George agreed. "I nearly collided with another skier over on the back slope."

"I'm ready to call it a day, too," Bess put in. "Let's go get hot chocolate and a doughnut."

"But we just had lunch," George groaned.

"I know," Bess said, "but still . . ."

"Hey, guys," Nancy interrupted them. "I never noticed those snowmobiles before. Look, right over there, next to the Queen's Tower." She pointed toward the far end of the castle, beside the round tower. Twenty or so snowmobiles sat parked in two rows, a few yards from the castle walls. Someone in a black snowmobile suit was brushing the snow off the windshield of one of them.

"Maybe we could go snowmobiling instead," George said eagerly. "That would be cool."

56

"Let's take these skis off, stash them in the lockers, change boots, and go take a look," Nancy said. "In this snowfall, maybe a snowmobile ride will be easier than skiing."

The girls quickly went to change their gear. But when they came out the doors from the locker room a few minutes later, there was no one near the snowmobiles.

"Who's in charge?" Bess asked as they crunched along the snowy path toward the snowmobiles. "I thought I saw someone over here before."

"Strange," Nancy said. "Whoever it was seems to have disappeared."

"Hey, neat," George said. She climbed onto a shiny red snowmobile and peered down at the dashboard. "The key is right here in the ignition. Maybe we're just supposed to jump on and go."

"Maybe we can," Nancy said uncertainly. "Still, I wonder where that guy went." She threaded through the rows of snowmobiles, heading toward the other side of the Queen's Tower. "Maybe he's around here," she said. She rounded the curved wall, leaving George and Bess behind.

Then Nancy halted in her tracks. About ten feet away, someone in a black snowmobile suit was standing beside the tower, tugging on something attached to the outside wall. Nancy's footsteps were muffled by the snow, and the person

57

seemed not to know she was there. She squinted through the falling snow, trying to see what the person was doing.

The bulky black snowmobile suit made it hard for Nancy to tell if it was a man or a woman. The snowmobile helmet totally hid his or her face, too. Nancy judged that the person was of medium height, but even that was hard to tell for sure.

What was this character tugging on so hard? Nancy wondered. Could this be an outside entrance to the Queen's Tower?

"Hey, Nancy!" George called around the corner. "You gotta see this thing! It's unreal!"

Startled by the sound of George's voice, the figure in black swung around, instantly spotting Nancy. Jerking away from the wall, whoever it was began to run through the falling snow toward the parked snowmobiles.

Nancy sprang forward, trying to grab a black-clad arm. But the person dodged her, and Nancy slipped, falling forward into a pile of snow.

Scrambling back to her feet, Nancy looked up to see the person jump onto the nearest snowmobile. George and Bess had just seen what was going on and were moving in that direction. But the figure in black had a pretty good head start.

He or she reached into the pocket of the bulky suit and pulled out a key. Nancy saw a shiny object also fall out of the pocket and into the snow.

The figure in black jammed the key in the

snowmobile ignition, and the engine roared to life. The girls were closing in from both sides, but they were still a few yards away.

Then the rider turned and gave the nearest snowmobile a fierce kick in Nancy's direction. The heavy blue snowmobile slid sideways, knocking Nancy to the ground. Her left leg sank into the snow beneath the heavy machine's runners!

She lay there helplessly, watching, while the rider in black roared away in a great whoosh of snow.

7

George's Chase

"Nancy, are you okay?" George called out as she and Bess hurried toward their friend.

"I think so," Nancy said. "But please get this snowmobile off me!"

Quickly the cousins ran to Nancy's side and struggled to lift the heavy machine. A moment later they heaved it back into its upright position. Nancy gingerly slid her leg to one side.

"You guys wait here—I'm going after that idiot," George declared. She swung onto another snowmobile, turned its ignition key, and gunned the engine. As she shifted it into gear, the snowmobile slid wildly to one side, but George quickly got it under control and roared off toward the woods.

"How does your leg feel?" Bess asked Nancy anxiously.

Nancy gave her leg a careful stretch. "It did

get banged pretty badly," she admitted. "Let's see if I can walk on it."

With Bess's help, Nancy raised herself onto her right leg. Then she set down her left foot and tested it. She winced but hobbled over to where the bright object had fallen from the black figure's pocket. "I thought I saw something," she murmured, leaning down looking in the snow.

"What is it?" Bess asked, catching up to her and leaning over her shoulder.

"It's a key," Nancy said, picking up the shiny shape and turning it over in her gloved hand. "A very large and old key."

"Hey, that rings a bell," Bess said, looking at Nancy.

"It sure does, Bess," Nancy said. "This looks just like the key Dexter Egan used last night to let Lisa out of the false staircase."

"Could this be the key that was in the lock when Lisa went in there?" Bess asked.

"It sure could be," Nancy said. "And the person who just buzzed off on that snowmobile dropped it. That makes me think it's the same person who locked Lisa in the stairway."

"Someone who's sure up to no good," Bess said. "Why did that wacko knock the snowmobile over on you?"

"I think I saw something that our friend didn't want anyone to see," Nancy said. "When I went around the corner, I saw that person pulling on something on the wall of the tower. It might be that secret entrance we were hoping to find."

"Let's go check it out," Bess said eagerly.

Leaning on Bess's shoulder, Nancy limped around the curving wall of the tower. Following footprints in the snow, they found the spot where the person in black had been standing.

Nancy crouched down to examine the footprints. "I can't tell much from these," she said to Bess. "The person was wearing thick, heavy boots. These footprints seem large, but with a couple pairs of socks on, even someone with small feet might be comfortable in boots this size."

Then Nancy stood up and ran her hand along the tower's stone wall. A thin layer of falling snow had blown against the stone, and small clumps of frozen ivy clung to the wall. But there was one tiny area, about four feet above the ground, that had been brushed bare. Nancy bent down to look at it more closely.

A small stone, rounded like a smooth mound, projected from the wall there. Nancy took off one glove and groped along the raised surface. "Maybe this is what our friend was yanking on," she said.

"Oh, Nancy, I bet it's a secret door handle!" Bess exclaimed.

Nancy wrapped her hand around the knob of stone and struggled to get a firm grasp. By grabbing it a certain way, it was possible to give it a tug. But when she tugged, nothing happened.

Bess gave a disappointed sigh. "No luck, huh?" she said.

Nancy straightened up. "If it does work, I can't figure out the trick," she confessed. "Maybe we can try it another time. But right now—" She paused. "You know, this leg really is starting to hurt. I don't want to make it worse by standing on it too long. Maybe I'd better go inside and give it a rest for a while."

"Oh, Nancy, you should have said something," Bess said earnestly. "You get off that foot right away."

Bess pulled Nancy's left arm around her shoulder to support her on that side. The two girls headed back toward the locker room doors, Nancy hobbling painfully.

"There is one other thing we need to check out, though, Bess," Nancy said as they made their way along the slippery path. "Could you take the key we just found and go up to the third floor? Stick the key in the lock and see if it works. That way we'll know for sure if it was the key to the false staircase."

"And then we'll know for sure that the black snowmobiler is the same person who locked up Lisa," Bess added.

Nancy gritted her teeth as they maneuvered down the steps to the locker room entrance.

63

"Only one problem," she said. "I just remembered—Mark asked Dexter to remove the lock on that door."

"That's right," Bess said. "If he's already done it, we may never know if it's the same key."

Nancy moved to a bench right by the locker room doors and dropped onto it. "Well, Mark and Christi should still have a copy of the key," she said. "If the lock has been removed, find them and see if this key matches theirs. Meanwhile, I'll sit here and keep an eye out for George."

Bess gave her a worried frown. "While I'm upstairs," she said, "how about if I hunt down Dr. Alvarez? Maybe she'll come take a look at your leg."

"Good idea, Bess," Nancy agreed, lifting her leg to stretch it out on the bench beside her. "But don't tell her exactly what happened—I don't want anyone to know about that mystery person we were chasing." She gave a wry smile. "I'll be waiting right here."

Bess took the key from Nancy, waved a mittened hand, and slipped inside through the door. Nancy leaned back against the wall of the castle and breathed deeply, trying to ease the pain in her leg.

In the distance she heard the roar of an engine. A moment later she saw George come charging out of the woods on her snowmobile, bumping along the surface of the snow. Nancy waved her arm to catch George's attention.

George steered over to the entrance, pulled up, and snapped off the ignition. "I looked everywhere for that jerk," she said in disgust as she climbed off the snowmobile. "But there was no sign anywhere. And there were so many other tracks in the woods, I couldn't even tell which way the snowmobile had gone."

Nancy heaved a sigh. "Tough luck," she said. "I really hoped you'd catch that character. It looks like he or she is involved in even more of the stuff that's been going on."

"Really?" George asked. She bounded down the steps to sit on the bench beside Nancy. "Like what?"

Nancy told George about finding the old-fashioned door key in the snow. "Bess has gone inside to check out whether it's the key that locked Lisa in the staircase," she said.

"What do you think this guy is up to, Nancy?" George wondered. "I mean, why would anyone want to lock Lisa up in a staircase? And what was the point of shoving that snowmobile over on you?"

"I can't answer your question about Lisa yet," Nancy said. "But I think I know why I got my leg crushed." She went on to tell George what she had seen the figure in black doing by the tower wall. Then she described what she and Bess had found on the wall.

"I'll bet it's the secret entrance, Nan," George said. "We have to go back and try it again. But not today. It looks like you need to go inside and get some help for that leg."

"Bess is trying to find Dr. Alvarez for me," Nancy said. "But I guess they can find us just as easily if we go inside here. I have to admit, the cold is starting to get to me." She shivered.

"Good idea," George said. "There shouldn't be anyone in the locker room at this time of day—everybody else is probably still out on the slopes."

George helped Nancy through the door and settled her onto a bench inside. They eased off Nancy's boot and rolled up the left leg of her pants. A huge purple bruise covered Nancy's shin, almost all the way up to her knee, and the skin was broken in a couple of places. Already, the bruised part was starting to swell up.

The two girls were bent over intently, examining Nancy's leg, when they heard the click of the outside door latch. They both looked up. "I guess someone else is coming in from the cold, too," George said.

With a burst of snow and wind, the door swung open. "Well, hello there, girls," said a booming male voice. "Great snow today, yes?"

The two girls gasped in disbelief.

It was Professor Hotchkiss—wearing a black snowmobile suit!

66

8

The Circular Stairs

With a cheerful wave, the professor paused to shake the snow off his black snowmobile outfit and heavy boots. Then he trudged across the locker room, heading toward the stairs to the main lobby.

"Professor Hotchkiss!" Nancy called out from the bench. "May we speak to you a moment?"

The professor turned and faced the girls. "Yes, of course, Nancy," he replied, puzzled.

"I just noticed your suit," Nancy said. "Have you been out snowmobiling?"

"Well, yes," he replied, looking uneasy. "Why do you ask?"

"A little while ago, we ran into someone over by the snowmobiles," Nancy said, carefully watching the reaction on his face. "We couldn't tell who it was, but the person was dressed in black, just like you are. Was it you?"

The muscles in the professor's face tightened. "No," he said curtly. "Whomever you saw, it was not I. No one was around when I went out on my snowmobile or when I returned. And I must say, I find it odd that you should ask me this."

"It may seem odd, Professor," Nancy said, "but it's crucial that we know who this person was."

"Why on earth?" the professor asked haughtily.

Nancy hesitated, her mind racing. What excuse could she give for her question? She couldn't let the professor know she was investigating a mystery.

Before she could answer, the sound of voices drifted down the stairs from the lobby. "That must be Bess and Dr. Alvarez," George said.

Nancy looked over to the steps, relieved to be interrupted. Seconds later Bess and the doctor walked into the locker room. "There she is," Dr. Alvarez said brightly. "Bess tells me a snowmobile accidentally fell on your leg, Nancy. Let me take a look at it."

Behind Dr. Alvarez, Nancy saw Bess staring openmouthed at the professor in his black outfit. The professor backed away, looking caged. Then he turned and hurried up the stairs without another word.

"Was he the one we saw?" Bess asked George in a low voice.

"He said it wasn't him," George murmured softly. "We'll tell you later."

Meanwhile Dr. Alvarez prodded at Nancy's injured leg with her skillful hands. "You have a bad bruise, Nancy," she finally said. "But I don't see any sign of a sprain or broken bones. I recommend you just give it as much rest as possible. Except for going to meals, stay off it tonight. Tomorrow you can walk around a bit, but don't try any sports. It should feel fine after that."

Nancy agreed and thanked her. Dr. Alvarez patted Nancy's leg, stood up, and said goodbye to the girls.

After the doctor had left, George suggested that they take the elevator upstairs. "You shouldn't climb those stairs, Nancy," she said. "And just because we got stuck once doesn't mean it'll happen again."

"I agree, it's worth the risk," Nancy said. With her friends' help, she limped down the corridor to the small elevator.

"What did you learn about the key?" Nancy asked Bess as they rode up.

Bess nodded happily. "It fits," she reported. "Dexter hadn't removed the lock yet. I pushed the key right in the hole and turned the lock."

"So the figure in black must be the same person who locked Lisa in the staircase," Nancy said.

69

"Do you think it's Professor Hotchkiss?" George asked.

"The person out there did seem to have a bulky build," Nancy said, "just like the professor. But whoever it was may have just layered a lot of clothes under the snowmobile suit. The person also seemed roughly the same height as the professor, but it's hard to judge with the helmet and the boots on."

"The professor doesn't seem like the type to push a snowmobile over on someone," Bess said. "He seems like all talk and no action."

"You never know," Nancy said. "And he does have a motive. With his interest in French history and Marie Antoinette, it figures that he'd like to find that tower room."

"But why would he lock Lisa in the stairs?" George asked as the elevator stopped—safely, this time, right at the third floor.

"I have to admit, I have no idea," Nancy said with a sigh. She pushed open the door. "But I'd still put him high on our list of suspects right now."

That night, long after dinner, the three friends sat in their room, going over the plans to the castle. "It's just as we thought," George was saying. "Here's the third floor. This is the corridor we went down Sunday night when we heard the hammering and the footsteps. See—it butts up against the round tower."

70

"But there's no doorway drawn at the end of the hall," Bess said.

"Mark and Christi had these plans drawn after they moved in," Nancy reminded her. "If the tower was already sealed up, a door wouldn't be shown there." She pulled out another sheet of plans. "Here's the plan for the lower level. I just wanted to check where that hallway leads to—the one from the locker room to the elevator."

She traced the blueprint with her finger. "It makes a few turns," Nancy said, "but after that, it straightens out and runs along this wall of the castle. But there are no rooms along it."

"Just like the corridor on the third floor," Bess commented. "Why would anyone build hallways like that?"

As they sat silently studying the plans, suddenly they heard familiar sounds in the distance. All three girls sat up, straining to listen.

"The thudding sounds," George said.

"Right," Nancy replied. "Coming from down the hall." She started to climb out of bed. "Let's go!"

"Nancy!" Bess said, holding her arm. "No way. Dr. Alvarez said you should rest that leg."

"Bess is right," George said, jumping up and grabbing some jeans. "You stay here. We'll check it out and then come tell you what we've found."

"Oh, all right," Nancy said with a sigh as she sank back on the bed. She hated to miss hunting down a clue, but she knew that the cousins were right. She really should give her leg a rest.

Her friends hurriedly threw on their clothes and slipped out of the room. Nancy restlessly went back to studying the plans.

She laid the pages for the lower level and the third floor next to each other. Carefully she compared the layouts of the two corridors. Hmm, she thought to herself. Both hallways ran along the same wall of the castle. In fact, they were located right on top of each other! Which meant that—

The doorknob turned, and the cousins ran in. "Nancy," Bess said breathlessly, dropping down on the edge of the bed, "we not only heard the thudding sounds, we heard the footsteps, too. They were going upstairs, then they faded away, just like before."

"If only we could find a way through that wall," George fretted.

"I think I know where we can find it," Nancy said. She swung her legs over the side of her bed and reached for her sweats.

"Nancy, you can't—" George started to say.

"Yes, I can," Nancy said. "I'll take it easy, I promise. But we have to get into that tower!"

"How?" Bess asked.

"By going down to the basement," Nancy said,

standing up and grabbing her penlight and her lock-picking kit. "That corridor downstairs leads right to the Queen's Tower, too. If there's an entrance anywhere, it would be down there, wouldn't it? Come on—it's time to find out."

They didn't hesitate to take the elevator to the basement. They knew there was no time to waste. When they stepped out downstairs, they turned in the opposite direction, away from the locker room. Nancy switched on her penlight so they could find their way down the pitch-dark corridor.

"Hey, guys," Nancy said at last, "another dead end." She ran the penlight's beam up and down a brown wood wall at the end of the hall.

"Do you think there's a door there?" George asked.

"Let's hope," Nancy said, approaching the wall. Her light soon picked out a small S-shaped door handle. "Wouldn't you know—it's locked," she reported. She rattled the knob and then took her lock-picking kit from her pocket. "Bess, shine the light on this lock," she said, handing her penlight to Bess.

After a few seconds of delicate manipulation, Nancy heard the tumblers fall into place. "I've got it!" she announced. She gave the door handle a turn and gently pushed the door open.

Cautiously the girls stepped into a small, windowless room about the size of a roomy closet.

"Hey, look at these walls," Bess said, shining the penlight around. "I never saw anything like that. What are all those carvings?"

Nancy stepped over and examined the carvings with her fingertips. "They're shaped like feathers," she said. "This entire wall is covered with thick carvings of wooden feathers."

"It sure is weird," Bess said, touching the intricate carvings. "Why would anyone make a wall like this?"

"Possibly to conceal something," Nancy murmured as she groped along the wall. "One of the best ways to hide something is to make it blend in with its surroundings."

"But what—?" George started to ask.

"Here we go!" Nancy interrupted. "This carving right here. See how it sticks out? I'll bet this is what we're looking for." Nancy gave the thick wooden feather a push.

A low humming sound rose from the back wall. The three girls spun around to face it, and Bess flashed the penlight that way. They saw an oak panel slowly rising, revealing a large, dark opening.

Taking the penlight from Bess, Nancy stepped inside the opening and ran the beam along a curved stone wall. "The inside of the Queen's Tower!" she said excitedly. "We've found it!"

"And will you look at those stairs," Bess said. A wooden, circular staircase wound along the curved wall, spiraling upward into the darkness.

"Come on, guys, let's go," Nancy said excitedly as she started up the first few steps.

"Be careful, Nan," George said. "Are you sure your leg can stand the climb?"

"I'll go slowly," Nancy promised.

"Well, don't lean on this railing too much," George warned, holding on to the frail banister. "It's pretty loose in places."

"I know. But we can't stop now," Nancy said as she climbed upward. "Watch out," she called back a moment later. "Some of these stairs are really rickety. You could go right through them."

As the girls climbed cautiously upward, they began to hear the familiar thudding sounds, faint at first but growing louder.

"We're on the right track," Nancy said softly, shining her beam ahead. "I think I can see the top of the stairs now. But I don't see any door up there."

"You're right, Nancy," George said. "It looks like those steps just go straight up and then stop."

"I hope this isn't another one of Ezra Wickford's dead ends," Bess said, looking uneasily back downward.

"There must be some sort of a door or exit up here," Nancy said firmly. She shone her light along the wall, running her fingers up and down the dusty surface. "There! That feels like a latch." She pushed hard with her free hand. A narrow door swung open.

The three girls stepped through the door and

onto a small, square landing. "Now we're much closer to that thudding sound," George remarked softly.

"Shhh!" Nancy pointed to a closed door straight ahead of them. A bright light streamed through the thin crack around its edges.

"Somebody's in there," Bess whispered. "And that's definitely where the noises are coming from."

Nancy nodded as she moved quietly toward the door with George and Bess close behind. Nancy put her hand on the ornate brass doorknob and gave it a gentle turn. The door swung slowly open.

Through the door the girls saw a dazzling round room, its walls covered with brilliant embossed gold. But their eyes flew immediately to the far side of the room. All three gasped in surprise.

A man crouched close to the wall, glaring at them, a hammer clutched menacingly in one hand.

It was Jacques Brunais!

9

The Secret Room

"What are you doing here?" Jacques Brunais asked sharply, straightening up. "How did you find this room? How did you get in the tower?" He tightened his grip on the hammer.

"Why don't you tell us why *you're* here?" Nancy said, wanting to get the upper hand. "And what are you doing to that wall?" She pointed to the wall behind him, where a small patch of the gold paneling had been pulled off.

"That's none of your business," Jacques spat out defiantly in his thick French accent.

"Mark and Christi asked us to investigate the strange noises they've heard at night," Nancy said. "We followed the noises, which led us here. They also asked us to find out who vandalized the library. What you're doing here sure looks like vandalism. Mark and Christi could bring criminal charges against you for this."

Nancy's bluff worked. Jacques's muscular body seemed to sag. "That could get me deported back to France," he said with a groan, dropping his eyes. He plopped down on a small stool next to his tools and buried his handsome face in his hands. "I had better tell you the whole story."

The three girls crossed the room to face him, waiting for his explanation.

"Back in the 1920s," Jacques began, lifting his head with a sigh, "Ezra Wickford—the man who built Wickford Castle—was traveling in France. He visited Chateau Rochemont, which was built long ago by a French duke and duchess. From people in town, Mr. Wickford heard that Marie Antoinette and her husband, King Louis XVI, used to visit the duke and duchess there. He became fascinated with the chateau, especially with this tower, where Marie Antoinette supposedly stayed during her visits."

"So he decided to buy the tower?" Bess asked.

"Yes," Jacques replied. "And he had the entire tower imported from France to Wisconsin. He wanted the tower to be exactly as it was when Marie Antoinette lived."

Jacques swept his arm around, showing off the round room's ornate gold walls. "Someone told him that this was Marie Antoinette's private writing room, designed just for her," the handsome skier went on. "Look closely at these walls. They are made of many small pieces, each carved like a tiny leaf and then coated with gold."

"They're beautiful," Bess said, reaching out gently to touch the wall beside her.

"Each piece was carved by hand, then mounted on thick wall panels," he explained, pointing to the spot on the wall where he had removed a few pieces. "See how each leaf fits tightly into its own place on the panel? They are like a jigsaw puzzle."

"It's incredible," George said, kneeling down to examine the intricate wall design.

"The crystal chandelier," Jacques went on, pointing toward the ceiling, "was put in for the queen, or so the story goes." The girls stared upward at an immense chandelier in the middle of the high ceiling. At least a hundred crystal pendants, now coated with dust, dangled from it. Its light bounced off the gilt walls and cast the whole room in a golden glow.

"In France it was lit by candles," Jacques told them. "When Mr. Wickford brought it here, he must have had it wired for electric lights instead. Only a few bulbs are in now, but when they are all there, imagine how the light would dazzle!"

From his tone of voice, Nancy could tell that Jacques loved this room. She realized that his threatening manner earlier had just been a scared reflex. He would never damage this beautiful place.

"Mr. Wickford must have loved this room," Bess said. "So why did he make it so hard to get in?"

"Maybe he wanted it as his own private refuge," Jacques said, shrugging. "All I know is, I had to explore every corridor before I found the stairs. And then it took more time to find the right carved feather to push."

"We were guided by the sound of your hammering," Nancy explained. "How did *you* know where to look? How did you even know this room was here?"

"That's another story," Jacques said. "You see, I grew up in a village near the French Alps, not far from Chateau Rochemont. In the 1920s, when the tower was taken apart, my great-grandfather was the master carpenter. He helped prepare it for shipment to America. There was no detail about it that he didn't know. He talked about it often through the years—about how beautiful it was. I loved hearing those stories when I was a boy."

"I can imagine," Bess said with a sigh. She settled herself on the floor by Jacques's feet, gazing up at his rugged, good-looking face.

"But there was one secret about the room that my great-grandfather told nobody," Jacques went on. "He told me the secret the night he died—me and no one else."

The girls sat quietly, scarcely daring to breathe, waiting for Jacques to go on.

"When he prepared this room for shipment to Wisconsin," Jacques said, "he had to take down the wall boards with the gold leaves attached.

80

Each board is about six inches thick, you see, so they are very heavy. While he was doing this, a loose gold leaf fell off its panel. Behind it, my great-grandfather found a small secret niche carved into the wall board. It had been hidden from view by the gold leaf. Tucked inside the niche was a bundle of letters tied up with a pink ribbon."

An excited little gasp escaped Bess.

"My great-grandfather untied the ribbon and looked at the letters," Jacques said, his gray eyes gleaming with the thrill of his story.

"What did the letters say?" Nancy asked.

"Unfortunately," Jacques said, "my great-grandfather, like so many working people of that time, could not read or write very well. But he felt sure that the letters had been written by Marie Antoinette. On the back of each one was the seal of a signet ring—a seal that he knew was the queen's crest. He had seen that crest on some old tapestries in the chateau."

"What did he do with the letters?" George asked.

"He was standing there, wondering what to do," Jacques said, "when some other carpenters came in the room. Before anyone could see him, he hid the bundle back in the niche and covered it up with the gold leaf. He planned to go back and get the letters the next day. But then an unfortunate thing happened."

"What was that?" Nancy asked.

"The next morning," Jacques said, "workers came in early and packed all the wall panels in big crates. When he arrived, my great-grandfather had no idea which wall panel the niche was in. They all looked so much alike. He went through many crates, searching for the panel with the secret niche. But he never found it. And the next day the crates were loaded onto wagons and taken away."

"How sad," Bess said softly.

"I don't think my great-grandfather ever got them out of his mind," Jacques said. "Finally, on his deathbed, he told this story to me, his favorite great-grandson. He asked me to promise that I would come here to America, to Wisconsin, and find the letters—and restore them to France."

"That's why you came to America?" George asked.

"Yes," Jacques replied. "It took a few years, but finally I saved up enough money to make the trip. Once I was in Wisconsin, it didn't take me long to find Wickford Castle. When I learned that it had become a ski lodge, I knew I was in luck. As an experienced skier, I was sure I could get a job here as a ski instructor."

"And during the evenings," Nancy said, "you searched for the secret room."

"Yes," Jacques said. "Finally I found it. Then I began my real search: looking for the letters. Night after night, I have been coming up here, taking each leaf one by one from the wall." He laid his hand on the gold carved wall. "If I do not see the niche, I put the leaf back and try another one. It seems like the job will never end, but I won't give up. I *know* the letters are here somewhere."

"But, Jacques," Nancy said, "what if someone else found them a long time ago? Like maybe one of the carpenters who reassembled the room when it first came here?"

"That is not likely," Jacques said. "When the room was reassembled, they only had to put the panels back on the walls. The gold leaves would not have been taken off. And obviously no repairs were made in later years." He pointed to tiny cracks in the leaves and places where the gold paint had flaked off. "This has not been touched for decades."

"No one else knows about the hidden letters?" Nancy asked. "No clues were left anywhere?"

"I do not know," Jacques admitted. "Mark and Christi say that the books in the library downstairs also came from Chateau Rochemont. They were all shipped over here along with the tower. I have wondered if any of those books contained clues."

"You mean if someone long ago left a note in a book about where the letters were?" Bess asked.

"Something like that," Jacques said. "I've looked through the library, hoping that I might find something. But I never have."

Nancy paused, thinking of the scattered books

downstairs. They had obviously been read recently. "Jacques," she asked gravely, "were you the one who ransacked the library?"

Jacques's handsome face flushed. "Definitely no!" he said. "Never would I harm those precious old books!"

Nancy didn't ask him about the gouged-out wall panel in the library. But she thought to herself that someone seemed to have been looking there for a niche—just like the niche that Jacques's great-grandfather had described to him.

"Did this tower have an outside entrance?" Bess asked Jacques. Following Bess's train of thought, Nancy remembered the figure in the black snowmobile suit, tugging on the stone in the tower wall.

Jacques frowned. "Not that I know of," he said. "But I did not look there."

The skier stood up. "Now I have told you my entire story," he said. "You are not going to report me to Mark and Christi, are you? I do not want to lose my job—and I do not want to be sent back to France." He clenched his fists at his sides. "Please, not until I have found the letters."

"We won't," Bess promised eagerly.

"Wait a minute, Bess," Nancy said. "Mark and Christi asked us to look into this case. We can't keep information from them." She studied Jacques's anxious face. "Instead of us telling Mark and Christi, what if you tell them yourself?

Explain the whole story as you did to us. Mark might even have some information that would help you in your search."

"I'll bet they'll understand, Jacques," Bess said, still gazing starry-eyed at him.

"If you three will go with me," Jacques said staunchly, "then I'll do it. Tomorrow morning, before breakfast."

"Great," Nancy said. "We'll meet you in the lounge about eight."

"Fine," Jacques said, following Nancy and her friends as they moved toward the door. "And thank you, girls, for being so kind."

"No problem, Jacques," Bess said, giving him an adoring smile. "Any time."

"Right," George said, clearing her throat and poking Bess in the back.

"Now I must put everything back in place. Be careful going down," Jacques said as he held the door open for them. "Those stairs are not very strong."

"We will, Jacques," Nancy said, snapping on her penlight. "Thanks."

With Bess and then George following close behind, Nancy led the way through the landing and down the steps. Her leg ached badly now, and she had to watch her footing. All three girls were silent as they climbed carefully downward.

"Are we almost there?" Bess whispered a few minutes later.

"I think so—that looks like the ground floor, right below us," Nancy answered softly.

"I don't know about you guys," George said, bringing up the rear, "but I'm ready to pack it in. It's been quite a—"

But George never finished her sentence. A sickening crunch of splintering wood filled the air, echoing through the walls of the empty tower. "Whoa! Help!" George called frantically.

Nancy whirled around, quickly flashing her light up the steps behind her. She was just in time to see George go crashing through the stairs—plunging straight for the floor below!

10

The Eavesdropper

"George! Quick!" Nancy called out as she saw her friend plunge through the tower's rickety stairs. "Grab something!"

George reached out and, with her right hand, swiftly grabbed a step just above her head. She teetered for a second as she struggled to hang on.

"Tight!" Nancy called, hobbling back up the steps. "Hang on tight!"

George tried to swing her left arm around to get a better hold on the broken stair. But the fingers of her right hand began to slip, and she swung wildly in midair.

Bess had already dropped to one knee on the step just below where George had crashed through. "George! Here!" she cried out, thrusting her arm into the gap. "Grab my hand! Quick!"

Still thrashing about, George clutched at Bess's hand with her left hand.

Kneeling beside Bess, Nancy reached down and grabbed George's right wrist. "We've got you, George," she said. "We'll pull you up."

Just then the step that Nancy and Bess were kneeling on shifted and gave an ominous creak. Nancy reached out for the wall, accidentally dropping her penlight. As it fell through the open stairs to the floor, they were plunged into darkness.

"No, don't pull me!" George said, gripping tight on their hands to steady herself. "I don't want you to crash through another stair. Besides, the edge of the wood there is all jagged. I can drop down to the floor below. It's not too far."

"Be careful, George," Bess said worriedly.

"I will," George said. "On the count of three, I want you to let go of me."

George took a breath and began. "One . . . two . . . three." Nancy and Bess let go of George's wrists. There was a beat of silence as George fell through the air. Then Nancy heard her drop with a thump onto the stone floor.

"Hey, I even landed on my feet!" George called up proudly from the darkness below.

Nancy and Bess scuttled down the rest of the stairs to join George. "Are you okay?" Nancy asked.

"Except for a couple of sore feet, yes," George answered. "That was some drop!"

"No joke!" Bess said. "That could have been quite an accident."

"Right," Nancy said. She spotted her penlight shining dimly as it lay on its side and picked it up. Training the beam on the broken step, Nancy gave a low whistle. "Maybe it wasn't an accident, George," she said grimly.

"What do you mean, Nancy?" Bess asked.

Nancy moved, limping, back up the stairs and ran her light along the sides of the cracked stair. "This wasn't caused by age or disrepair," she reported. "This step has been sawed!"

"Sawed?" George called from below. "You mean somebody made me fall on purpose?"

"It sure looks that way," Nancy said. "There's a fresh cut on the side—a clean, straight cut."

"But who—" Bess said.

"I don't know, Bess," Nancy said, turning and coming slowly back down the stairs. "But it seems like someone knew when we went upstairs. Someone rigged that step, hoping that one of us would fall through on the way up or down."

"Well, I think we've all had enough of this place," George said, heading through the open panel that led into the tiny room.

"But wait!" Bess said. "What about Jacques?"

"What *about* Jacques?" George asked, puzzled.

"She's right," Nancy said. "He has to be warned about the step."

The girls decided that Bess and George would

go back up the tower to tell Jacques to be careful on the stairs. Nancy waited for them at the bottom.

When they came back down, Bess said, "Let's get out of here."

"I'm with you," Nancy said.

They went back into the tiny room, and George opened the door into the long corridor, and they all passed through.

"This hall is so creepy," Bess said as the three headed down the dark basement corridor.

"Well, hang in there," George said. "We don't have far to go now."

"Shhh!" Nancy said suddenly, halting and snapping off her penlight. The girls crowded together, listening intently. "Down the hall," Nancy whispered. "Someone's coming from the locker room!"

The girls stood without breathing, listening to the soft footsteps that moved slowly toward them, coming around the corner from the elevator.

A moment later a light flashed in their eyes. The three girls squinted directly into the blinding beam of a flashlight.

"What're you girls up to?" a man's voice snarled behind the light. "What do you think you're doing here?"

Nancy took a small step forward, shielding her eyes with one hand. Once out of the direct beam, she could see who held the flashlight.

Dexter Egan!

"We're here to investigate some strange noises," George began to explain. "Mark and Christi—"

"Never mind, George," Nancy interrupted. "Why are you roaming around at this hour of the night, Mr. Egan?"

"I'm the caretaker!" Egan retorted indignantly. "It's my job to check on things." Then he stopped, cocking his grizzled head to one side. "What's that?" he asked nervously, flashing his light past the girls and down the dark corridor.

In the distance they could hear footsteps heading toward them. A moment later Jacques walked into the light.

"Hello again, girls," Jacques said as he approached the group. "Hello, Dexter." He paused, taking in the scene. "Don't tell me—I'll bet you met the girls here and thought they were up to something."

Dexter shrugged and said nothing, though he squinted one eye suspiciously.

"Don't worry, okay, Dexter?" Jacques went on. "These girls are friends of mine. Good friends."

Dexter mumbled something, but he turned and left them, retreating back around the corner.

"I'm not completely sure about him," Jacques said in a low voice once Dexter was out of earshot. "But he sure does know a lot about Wickford Castle after working here for thirty years. He's been very helpful to me."

"How much does he know about your search?"

Nancy asked as they walked down the hall toward the ski lockers.

"Not everything," Jacques replied, "but he knows more about it than I would like. One night a few weeks ago, Dexter found me working up in the tower room. Since he knows the castle so well, he wanders around everywhere. He asked why I was there. I had to tell him something, so I said I was searching for some papers that I thought were hidden there. I didn't tell him what the papers were."

"Did he offer to help?" Bess asked.

"No," Jacques replied. "But I did convince him to give me a key for the door to the tower stairs. I was getting tired of picking that lock every night. I took a while to talk him into it. He was afraid that Christi and Mark would find out, but I convinced him it was okay."

So that must have been the argument that Meg overheard Saturday night in the second-floor hallway, Nancy thought.

They reached the locker room, and Bess let out a sigh of relief. Nancy couldn't see Dexter Egan anywhere, so she asked Jacques another question that was on her mind.

"Yesterday, when we were checking out the library, someone was hiding behind the drapes," she said. "It turned out to be Dexter. Do you have any idea why he would be hiding there?"

"No," Jacques said with a shrug.

"Do you think he was the person who vandalized the library?" Nancy asked. "It was vanda-lized sometime after lunch on Saturday."

Jacques frowned. "I don't think so," he said. "He acts very, how you say, shifty. But I don't think he was the vandal." He turned toward the ski school office. "I still have some work to do in here. But I'll see you girls first thing tomorrow."

"Great," Nancy said. "We'll meet you in the lounge at eight o'clock."

"Au revoir," Jacques said, and with a wave, he disappeared inside the ski school office.

"So," George said, once the girls were back in their room, "I guess the mystery has been solved. Jacques will explain to Mark and Christi tomor-row what he's been up to, and they won't worry about those strange noises at night anymore."

"But that *doesn't* solve everything," Nancy said, stretching out on her bed. Her leg was aching badly, and she leaned forward and care-fully tucked a pillow under it. "We still don't know who vandalized the library. Was it Jacques, Dexter, or someone else? And who trapped us in the elevator that first day, George? Who locked Lisa in the staircase? And who was the person in black out by the tower today?"

"That couldn't have been Jacques," Bess de-clared. "He wouldn't be looking for an outside entrance. He already knows a way into the tower."

"So does Dexter," George pointed out.

"Maybe Jacques isn't the only person who's

hunting for the letters," Nancy said slowly. "What if someone else learned about them in some other way—like from one of the books in the library?"

"Those letters could be very valuable—more than Jacques realizes," George said. "Someone may want to publish them."

"True," Nancy said. "Of course, Jacques himself may know more than he's letting on. We still don't know him very well. We should keep watching him."

"Nancy," Bess said, "you can't suspect Jacques. He wouldn't do anything wrong. Jacques is too—"

"Look," Nancy said, interrupting her. "All we know for sure is that someone at Wickford Castle is determined to find the queen's letters. Whoever it is will do anything to avoid discovery—even harm us. From now on we must be suspicious of everyone."

On Wednesday morning Nancy slipped into hunter green stirrup pants with a bright red down vest layered over a white turtleneck. The cousins wore jeans with colorful ski sweaters. When they got downstairs, Jacques was waiting for them in the lounge, dressed in black ski pants and a burgundy sweater. A soft, admiring sigh escaped from Bess as he stood to join them.

Jacques and the girls headed straight for Mark and Christi's office. Nancy knocked on the door.

"Good morning, folks," Mark said cheerfully as he opened the door. He seemed a bit surprised, though, to see Jacques with Nancy and her friends. "How can we help you?"

"We need to talk to you and Christi," Nancy said. "It's important."

"No problem," Mark said. "Come on in."

As the four young people filed in, Gus left his favorite spot in the morning sun to sit next to Nancy. Christi looked up from the computer screen, where she was typing in room reservations. "Hi, everyone," she said brightly. "Have a seat."

Mark propped the door open and then seated himself at the keyhole desk. "So what's going on?" he asked.

"Something has come up," Nancy said, perching on a windowsill and gently scratching Gus's ear. "I think Jacques can explain."

Jacques found a chair, cleared his throat, and began. First he explained about the nighttime noises, then he went on to tell the story of his great-grandfather's secret.

Everyone was leaning forward intently to hear Jacques's quiet, husky voice. But then, out of the corner of her eye, Nancy saw something moving just outside the partly opened office door. She turned and looked over her shoulder toward the hall. Beside her, Gus raised his head and bristled.

She saw nothing but a shadow thrown by the

morning sun against the corridor wall. As Nancy watched, the shadow moved slightly, then stopped. It was clearly a person crouching by the office door.

Nancy turned quickly to Jacques and raised her finger to her lips to silence him. But he was so caught up in his tale, he didn't notice. ". . . and there he found a bundle of letters tied with a pink ribbon," Jacques was saying.

Nancy jumped to her feet. Someone was in the hall listening! Someone had heard the secret!

11

The Skating Party

Nancy slipped over to the door and peered out. Gus pushed past her with a low growl, looking alertly up the hall.

At the far end Nancy saw the shadow of a figure disappearing around the corner. Her muscles coiled to give chase, but then she relaxed. Her leg was in no condition for running, she realized, and the person had a head start.

But who could it have been? Nancy asked herself as she limped back into the office and sat down. Who had been eavesdropping on them—and why?

Wrapped up in Jacques's story, the others hadn't even noticed Nancy leave. "This is incredible," Mark was saying. "I can't believe there's really something of value hidden in the tower room."

97

"But, Mark," Bess said, "you yourself brought up the subject at dinner Sunday night."

Christi made a rueful face. "Mark always tells that story," she said. "But the truth is, he doesn't really believe it. It's just some local lore we learned from the neighbors. Mark likes to intrigue the guests with it."

"That's right," Mark said with an embarrassed chuckle. "It sort of makes this place seem more romantic, that's all."

That ruled out Mark and Christi as suspects, Nancy thought. They would never draw attention to the Queen's Tower if they really did think something valuable was hidden there.

"Anyway," Mark went on, "it's okay to go on looking, Jacques—just try to keep the noise down. Who knows? Maybe you *will* find the queen's letters."

"Wouldn't that be great," Christi said happily. "Something like that would really put Butter Ridge Winter Sports Area on the map."

"It sure would," Mark said. "Thanks, Nancy, for solving the mystery."

"I'm glad we could help," Nancy said. "But we still need to learn who vandalized the library and why. If it's okay, I'll keep on investigating."

Leaving the office, Jacques said goodbye and ran down to the ski school office to get ready for the day's lessons. The girls headed to the dining room for the buffet breakfast. Large platters were set out on the long center table, with scrambled eggs, bacon, and blueberry pancakes with hot Wisconsin maple syrup. Guests served themselves, then sat down at small tables set by the arched windows on the long side wall.

With a tall stack of pancakes on her plate, Bess led the way to an empty table. As Nancy followed, threading through the tables, her sharp ears picked up a man's voice saying, ". . . what the book says about Marie Antoinette is that she had—"

Then the voice broke off. Nancy's eyes darted over to see Lisa Ostrum and Professor Hotchkiss at a nearby table. The professor was glaring up at her, aware that she had overheard him.

Acting casual, Nancy walked on to her table. From the corner of her eye, she saw Lisa and the professor lean closer together to carry on their intense conversation.

Could Professor Hotchkiss have been the eavesdropper in the hall? she wondered. And what book was he talking about? One of the books in the castle's library?

"Did you guys notice someone listening outside the door while we were in the office?" Nancy asked as she sat down with Bess and George.

"No," Bess said. "Who was it?"

"I'm not sure," Nancy said. "I only saw a shadow in the hallway. But I know someone was

99

there. Gus noticed it, too. And it was right in the middle of Jacques's story—the most important part."

Bess's eyes widened. "Oh, no," she said softly. "Now someone else knows what's in the tower!"

Nancy nodded. "Whoever gouged that hole in the library wall already knew there was a treasure to find," she mused. "Maybe this is the same person—or maybe we've got a new suspect looking for the queen's secret. One more person to watch out for."

Just then Meg Alvarez came up to their table. "Are you guys going down for your lessons?" she asked.

"Bess and I are," George said. "But your mom told Nancy to stay off her leg today."

"Oh, that's right," Meg said. "She told me you had a run-in with a snowmobile, Nancy. How's it feeling?"

Nancy decided not to mention that she'd been prowling around the castle last night instead of resting her leg. "I'd better not try skiing today," she said. "After lunch I thought I'd drive into the village and check out some shops."

Bess's eyes lit up. "Great idea, Nan. Can I come along?"

"Me, too?" Meg chimed in. "I'd love to find something cool to wear to the skating party Mark and Christi have set up for tonight."

Nancy laughed. "The more, the merrier," she

agreed. "Why don't you come, too, George? One afternoon off the slopes won't hurt."

"What a neat shop!" Bess said that afternoon as the girls walked out of a clothing boutique, loaded down with shopping bags. "I love my new stretch pants."

"They looked great on you, Bess," Meg said.

"If I wear them to the skating party, do you think Jacques will notice?" Bess asked.

"Of course he will," Nancy said.

"Unless, of course, he's too busy noticing me," Meg said, playfully fluffing her shiny brown hair.

Bess stopped and gazed across shop-lined Main Street, the heart of the small resort town. "Hey, guys, look at that old-fashioned soda shop," she said. "How about stopping for a milkshake?"

"Bess!" George groaned. "A milkshake will definitely not help you look good in stretch pants."

But Bess was already heading across the street. The other girls followed her over to the quaint soda shop with its bright striped canopy. Inside, wooden booths ran along one wall. A marble-topped counter with high chrome stools took up the other wall.

An older woman in a pink uniform stood behind the counter. "Hello," she said as the girls climbed up onto stools. "What I can get for you today?"

101

"I'll have a chocolate shake," Bess said. "And a piece of that pecan pie." She pointed to a gooey brown pie in a glass-topped case beside her. George cleared her throat, but Bess ignored her.

"Good choice, dear," the woman said. "I made it myself. You'll love it."

"Homemade?" Meg asked. "Then I'll have a piece, too." Nancy and George ordered hot chocolate.

"Are you here to visit our new winter sports area?" the woman asked as she set their orders in front of them.

"We sure are," George said. "It's a super area. The slopes are great, and we love the lodge."

"Oh, you're staying at Wickford Castle?" the woman said. "The Lanes have done a grand job of fixing it up, I hear. I hope they make a go of it. Lots of local folks work up there—folks who wouldn't have had jobs otherwise. Like poor old Dexter Egan. He deserves a break after the rough time he's had."

Nancy sat up straight, intrigued. "Rough time? What do you mean, Mrs. Cole?" she asked, reading the woman's name from her black plastic name tag.

"Oh, he was always getting into trouble, that boy," Mrs. Cole said. "I never saw such a child."

"What kind of trouble?" Nancy asked.

"Playing hookey from school, shoplifting, things like that," Mrs. Cole said. "Then when he got older, there was a string of burglaries in town, and Dexter was charged with them. He ended up spending ten years in prison. But he's been out a couple years now, and he really seems straightened out. And thanks to Mark and Christi, he has a decent job."

Nancy quirked an eyebrow. "But I thought Dexter was caretaker at Wickford Castle for years," she said. "He sure knows the place inside out."

Mrs. Cole folded her arms. "Wickford Castle was abandoned for nearly twenty years," she said. "Young hoodlums used to sneak onto the grounds and prowl around. No one was there to stop them. No, Dexter, never worked there until six months ago." She gave a firm nod, then moved off to wait on another customer.

After she left, Nancy traded glances with her friends. "So Dexter Egan lied to Mark and Christi about his past," she said softly. "I wonder what else he's been lying about?"

After dinner that night, Bess stood in front of the mirror in their room, checking out her new stretch pants. "Are you sure you're up to skating, Nancy?" she asked.

Nancy pulled on an anorak. "My leg feels great," she said. "But if it starts hurting, I promise I'll leave the ice."

A quick knock came on the door, and George let in Meg Alvarez. "Hi, guys," Meg Alvarez said. "Everyone ready for the party?"

"Just about," Bess said, picking up her parka. "Hey, Meg, I love that purple stocking cap you have on. It looks like—"

"I know," Meg said, interrupting her, flipping the cap's long tassel. "It's Jacques's. My cap blew off into the woods this morning, so Jacques let me use his."

"Lucky you!" Bess said with envy.

The four girls trooped downstairs and joined other guests heading outside for the skating pond. As they rounded the corner of the castle, they saw a huge bonfire crackling by the pond's edge. Loudspeakers mounted below the floodlights blared pop music, and several people were already skimming across the ice.

"The pond's bigger than I realized," Nancy observed as they followed the path down a snowy slope. "Even all those lights don't light up the whole thing. See the part that curves back into the woods? It's awfully dark that way."

"So don't skate over there," George said. "There's plenty of space just on this end."

The four girls sat on benches by the bonfire to put on their skates. "Hi, guys," Lisa Ostrum said, gliding past them on the ice. She executed a neat spin, then sped away.

"Wouldn't you know, she's as good a skater as she is a skier," George commented.

"Hi, Mom," Meg called out, waving as Dr. Alvarez skated by with Professor Hotchkiss.

Skates on, the four girls moved onto the ice. Nancy tested her leg, and it felt fine.

"Bon soir, everyone," a familiar voice called out. Jacques, wearing a bright plaid parka, came up and circled around the girls. "Hey, Meg, love your hat!" he said, reaching over and playfully plucking his purple stocking cap off Meg's head.

"Hey, come on!" Meg called, laughing. Swinging the cap by the tassel, Jacques headed toward the far end of the pond with Meg in hot pursuit.

"I guess Jacques really likes Meg," Bess said forlornly, gazing after them.

Nancy and George each grabbed one of Bess's hands, forming a chain to whip around the ice. "Guys, guys, not so fast!" Bess was soon shrieking and laughing.

A playful voice from behind called out, "Mademoiselle!" Bess looked around. Jacques, without his purple cap again, swung in front of her and bowed. "You will do me the honor?" He held out his arm, and with a delighted giggle, Bess took it. The two skated off across the pond.

Leaving Bess alone to enjoy Jacques's attention, George and Nancy skated around the well-lit part of the ice, enjoying the music and the clear, crisp night air. Then they noticed Christi setting up a kettle of hot mulled cider by the bonfire. They joined the other guests gathering there to warm up.

Dr. Alvarez and Professor Hotchkiss were sitting on a bench, cradling warm mugs in their hands. "Isn't Meg with you?" the doctor asked Nancy and George.

George shrugged. "Last time we saw her, she was racing Jacques to the end of the pond."

"Well, she'll be back soon," Dr. Alvarez said, gazing across the pond as she sipped her cider.

Minutes passed, and more people gathered by the bonfire. The pond looked empty, and Meg still hadn't shown up. "Perhaps we should skate down near those woods and look for Meg," Professor Hotchkiss said.

Jacques, who had just skated up with Bess, frowned. "Meg?" he repeated. "She has not returned? I left her up near the woods—"

Nancy was already heading for the ice, her instincts on alert. Calling Meg's name, she zipped across the pond, heading for the far end.

Soon a dark shape on the ice, close to the pond's edge, caught her eye. She swerved toward it with a sinking feeling in her stomach. Nancy skidded to a stop, staring down in horror.

It was Meg, sprawled unconscious on the ice!

12

Stranded!

"Quick!" Nancy called. "Dr. Alvarez! Jacques! Someone, help!"

With a clang of skates, Dr. Alvarez arrived right behind Nancy. She knelt down anxiously on the ice. "Meg! What happened?" she asked as she raised her daughter's head and felt for her pulse.

George skated up breathlessly with Jacques and Bess close behind. "Is Meg okay?" she asked.

"I'm not sure," Dr. Alvarez said. "But we must get her out of this cold and over to the bonfire."

"Here," Jacques said, bending down. "Let me help." He gently lifted Meg's tall, limp body. With her safely in his arms, he skated back to the bonfire.

"Meg? Please open your eyes," Dr. Alvarez said urgently as she settled by the fire, cradling Meg in her arms. Squatting beside her, Lisa

Ostrum rubbed one of Meg's mittened hands in her own.

Meg opened her eyes and stared, confused, at the skaters gathered around her. "What happened?" she asked weakly. "Why is everybody . . . ?"

"You had an accident, Meg," Nancy said. "Down at the end of the pond. Do you remember what happened?"

Meg blinked and looked at Nancy. "I was skating along," she began. "Then everything went black and . . . that's all I remember."

"She's got a big lump here," Dr. Alvarez said, pulling off the purple stocking cap to examine the top of Meg's head. "It may have been caused by her fall—or she could have been hit by something."

Who would want to hurt Meg? Nancy wondered to herself. Automatically, she picked up Jacques's stocking hat. Then, looking down at the cap in her hand, a thought struck her.

Could someone have mistaken Meg for Jacques? she wondered. Meg *had*, after all, been wearing Jacques's distinctive purple cap.

Nancy stuffed the cap in her pocket and knelt down beside Meg. "Meg, did you see anyone nearby before you fell?" she asked.

"Someone may have been coming across the ice," Meg said as she rubbed her eyes and slowly sat up. "But it was really dark. I don't know who it was."

"Was it a man or a woman?" George asked.

"I honestly don't know," Meg said.

"We should get Meg inside," Dr. Alvarez said, standing up. "She needs some rest." Jacques and Professor Hotchkiss hurried forward to help carry the girl.

"Go in through the locker room and take her upstairs in the elevator," Christi suggested. She took off running to open the doors for them.

"I'll carry Meg's skates," Lisa offered. Bringing up the rear, she followed the group back toward the lodge.

The other guests huddled near the fire in small groups, talking about the incident. "Hey, guys," Nancy said softly to Bess and George. "Let's take a quick swing down to the end of the pond. We can search for any weapon that might be lying around."

"Good idea," George said. The three went back on the pond and skated over into the dark area.

"I don't see any weapon," George said as they scanned the ice. "But suppose someone hit her with a rock, then threw it off into the trees afterward."

"If that's what happened, we'll never find it," Bess said, gazing wearily into the dark woods.

Nancy sighed. "Even if we did, we wouldn't know which rock it was," she pointed out. "Meg didn't bleed, so it wouldn't show any bloodstains. I guess we'd better give up."

"Do you suspect someone, Nancy?" George asked as they turned and skated back.

"No one definite," Nancy said. "Dexter Egan could have been lurking in the woods nearby. We know Professor Hotchkiss was at the pond."

"We do know that Jacques skated across the pond with Meg," Bess said slowly. "I guess that makes him a suspect, huh, Nan?"

"Possibly," Nancy said. "Except that I think whoever hit Meg was really trying to get Jacques instead. Think about it. Meg is nearly as tall as Jacques, and they were both wearing dark ski parkas. And Meg was wearing his purple cap at the time."

Bess looked relieved. Then George said, "Unless Jacques hit Meg to make it look like *he's* a target—you know, to throw suspicion off himself."

"That's getting pretty farfetched," Nancy said, swinging toward the pond's shore and the welcoming bonfire. "But frankly, I'm not sure of anything anymore. We'll have to keep our eyes open. And tomorrow I'll talk to Jacques and find out what, if anything, he knows."

"It feels good to be out on the slopes again," Nancy said Thursday morning as she, Bess, George, and Meg trooped across the snowy field. "I'm glad to be back to normal."

"Me, too," Meg said. "I was afraid my mom

would make me rest today. But the lump on my head went down last night, so she said I could ski."

"You guys go up on the lift," Nancy said as they approached the triple chair lift. "I see Jacques coming. I'll ride up with him."

"Lucky you!" Bess said with a smile before following George and Meg toward the lift.

"Glad to see you on your skis again, Nancy," Jacques said as he met Nancy. "And how is my other pupil, Meg?"

"Just fine," Nancy said. "What a nasty accident, though. When you were skating with Meg, did you see anything suspicious?"

"Not really," Jacques said. "But then it was so dark there. By the way, did you find my cap?"

"Sure did, Jacques," Nancy said, pulling the purple cap out of her pocket and handing it to him.

"I don't know whether to wear this or not," Jacques said, fingering the cap's long tassel. "For all I know, whoever hit Meg thought she was me."

"I wondered that, too," Nancy said. She was surprised that Jacques had come up with the same theory. "But why would anyone want to hurt you?"

"To scare me off my search for the letters?" Jacques suggested, heading for the ski lift. "I cannot imagine any other reason. But then I can't think why anyone would want to hurt Meg either. And I'd feel very bad if she was hurt because of me."

After their lessons with Jacques, the girls ate a quick lunch and then went back out to the slopes. But late that afternoon, a frigid wind picked up from the north. The temperature dropped fast.

"I'm going to call it a day," Bess finally said. "This cold is too much for me."

"One more run down the racing trails, and I'll be ready, too," Meg said. "How about it, George?"

"I'm with you, Meg," George said, and the two girls took off for some final racing practice.

"I think I'll stay out a bit longer, Bess," Nancy said. "I'm going to ski some of the runs over on the back of the mountain."

"Have fun," Bess said with a wave as she headed down the mountain's front toward the lodge.

Many of the skiers from the village had already left on their shuttle bus, and the slopes were delightfully uncrowded. On her next run, Nancy did spot some guests from the castle—Professor Hotchkiss, Lisa Ostrum, Dr. Alvarez, and the Hills—but otherwise, there weren't many people out. By late afternoon only a few skiers were left braving the cold.

Reaching the base on the back side of the mountain, Nancy headed over to the lift. Here on the back of the mountain, there was only a single-person chair, not a triple-seat lift as there was on the front. "You'll be the last skier today," the lift attendant told her, swinging open the metal lap bar on the lift chair. "Time to close the slopes."

"Okay by me," Nancy said. "It's really cold."

"It's already zero," he said, nodding toward the thermometer fastened to the front of the tiny attendant's hut. "And that wind . . ." He gave a slight shudder as he held the lift chair for her. "When you get to the top, tell the attendant there that you're the last skier. Then he'll know it's time to close down the lift."

"Will do," Nancy called over her shoulder as the lift chair swung upward. The cable high above slid smoothly along its tracks, carrying the metal chair toward the top of the mountain.

A bone-chilling wind whipped through the pines and across the slopes. As the lift whisked her higher and higher above the ground, Nancy wrapped her arms around herself, trying to keep warm. She was definitely ready to go in, she decided. Once she reached the top, she would head directly down the mountain's front and into the warmth of the lodge. Her feet felt like ice, and she wiggled her toes, trying to keep warm.

The top of the mountain had just come into view when the lift jerked to a stop. Oh, no, Nancy thought. She peered over her shoulder toward the attendant's hut at the bottom. A stopped lift usually meant someone had slipped while getting on. But who would be getting on the lift now?

113

The attendant had said that she was the last skier of the day.

She stared down toward the lift station again, trying to figure out what had happened. But the hut area was dark now, and the attendant was nowhere to be seen.

Maybe someone fell getting off at the top, she thought. She looked up toward the mountain's top, but dusk was gathering fast. She could see nothing except for one empty chair way ahead of her, swinging from the lift cable.

An arctic blast whipped across the back of the mountain. Nancy's chair lurched wildly. Fighting a growing sense of panic, Nancy again looked over her shoulder toward the dark attendant's hut at the base. Then she turned and squinted up toward the top. Another gust of wind came through the pines, and her chair swayed noisily from side to side.

If she called out for help, she thought, someone might hear her. Even though she could see no one on the back of the mountain, it was still worth a try. She sat up straight and took a deep breath.

"Help!" she shouted loudly. She listened expectantly. All she could hear was wind whistling through the pines and the creak of the chair as it swung from side to side. "Help!" she called again. But she heard nothing but the wind.

Nancy peered anxiously up and down the slope. There was no sign of life anywhere. She was well out of sight of the lodge on the other side of the mountain.

She had to face facts, Nancy realized with a sinking sense of dread. Everyone else had gone in. She was stranded on the lift, perhaps for the whole night—in the deadly cold!

13

The Intruder

Don't panic, Nancy told herself as she huddled on the ski lift, struggling to keep warm in the frigid winter air. If she wanted to survive, she had to keep a clear head and consider her options.

For one thing, she reminded herself, sooner or later George and Bess would notice she was missing. They'd be sure to organize a search party. If she just stayed on the lift and kept calling out for help, eventually someone would come and find her.

She sat waiting for ten minutes or so as icy gusts whipped around her. No, Nancy told herself at last through chattering teeth, waiting up here for help was out of the question. It was too cold. She couldn't withstand the weather that long. Night was falling fast, and it would only get colder.

A second choice, she thought, was to try to climb off the lift. She leaned forward and peered down, trying to figure out how far above the ground she was. It had to be at least twenty feet, she judged—as high as a second-story window. Still, a jump might be possible.

But then she felt her skis weighing down her feet. It would be awfully risky to jump with them on, Nancy realized. If they got tangled in midair, she would fall head over heels down the slope.

Bending over, she tried to see if she could reach the bindings that attached her skis to her boots. Maybe she could snap off the bindings and let the skis drop off. But with the lift chair's lap bar in front of her, she couldn't reach her boots. And if she swung open the bar to bend over, she could fall right out—head first.

She tried to lift one foot high enough for her to undo the binding while sitting up. But with the ski and boot on, her foot was too heavy.

That left just one choice, Nancy concluded: to jump off the lift with the skis on her feet. As she dropped, she'd just have to keep them straight. If she could land upright, she'd be able to ski to a stop, take off her skis, and hike up over the mountaintop and down the front to the lodge.

By now, almost half an hour had passed, and a small sliver of moon appeared in the sky. In the fading light, Nancy examined the lift chair. One long metal pipe attached it to the cable overhead. Then, like an upside-down Y, it came down

117

and branched into two pipes, which were bolted to either side of the chair.

The best strategy, she decided, was to grab hold of one of the branching pipes on either side. She could dangle from the pipe and then jump. She suddenly became aware of the ski poles she was clutching in one fist. I can't do it while I'm holding these, Nancy realized. Well, I'll just have to try skiing without them. She heaved the ski poles off into the nearby pines.

Twisting sideways, Nancy grasped the metal pipe at the right side of her chair. Then, facing sideways and still tightly gripping the metal pipe, she scooted her hips forward. With her left hip, she nudged open the metal lap bar. She drew a deep breath, then pushed off from the chair.

Hanging onto the pipe tightly, Nancy felt her body skew around as the chair suddenly tipped forward. She dangled perilously in midair.

A gust of wind caught the chair, spinning it recklessly around. Nancy clung fiercely to the metal pipe as she mentally rehearsed her next move. She must land flat, Nancy reminded herself, or she'd go tumbling down the mountain. But right after landing, she'd have to throw her weight onto her strong right leg. Her injured left leg might crumple beneath her.

She closed her eyes, took a big breath, and let go. Her body skimmed through the air, picking up speed rapidly. Looking down, she saw the snowy ground rush up toward her.

Whomp! Nancy landed hard on both skis. She immediately shifted her weight to the right. But her timing was a split second off, and she started to skid. She was heading out of control, straight down the slope, with no ski poles to steady herself!

Nancy's arms waved like windmills as she fought to regain her balance. She was moving fast, struggling against the wind and icy snow to stay upright. She rotated her body to face across the slope, her right ski toward the bottom of the hill. Then she threw all her weight onto the right leg.

Immediately, she regained her balance. But she didn't have time to regroup. Better start turning right now, she told herself, or you'll go right into those pine trees in front of you!

Quickly she shifted her weight once more and swung gracefully around, churning to a stop. Thank heavens! Nancy thought as she stood still, trying to catch her breath. She was finally safe.

Or was she? She looked warily around. Here she was in the subzero cold, in the dark, halfway down the back of the mountain. She still had to hike to the top of the mountain and down the other side. The danger was far from over.

Well, first things first, she told herself briskly. Time to take off the skis. She'd stow them next to a tree, and then she'd start up the mountain.

But as she bent down to release her bindings, Nancy heard a rustling in the nearby woods. She straightened up and stared uneasily into the darkness.

In the moonlight, she saw a rapidly moving form. Something or someone was heading toward her!

She crouched down low in the snow and peered into the dark. She waited silently, not moving. Who or what was it? she wondered. How could she protect herself?

A moment later a shaggy form rushed out of the woods straight at her. Nancy tensed up.

But it was Gus, the sheepdog! He came charging across the snow like a tan streak, tail wagging like mad. Nancy, giddy with relief, threw open her arms, and he came bounding into them. Nancy pulled him to her in a giant hug.

In the distance, she heard the hum of an engine. Looking up toward the top of the mountain, she saw a single bright headlight coming directly toward her. A snowmobile!

Nancy halted uneasily, thinking about the stealthy snowmobile driver she'd met two days ago. But as the snowmobile got closer, she saw that it was driven by a member of the ski patrol coming to rescue her. Over the roar of the engine, a young woman swung around and called to Nancy to hop on.

Nancy stuck her skis into the snow next to a nearby tree and climbed on. Gus jumped on Nancy's lap. Nancy braced herself as the driver revved the snowmobile motor, shifted gears, and took off. They circled around and headed up the back of the mountain.

A few minutes later, the ski patroller pulled the snowmobile up in front of the ski school entrance. The locker room doors sprang open, spilling out light on the snow. A small crowd of skiers rushed out to greet Nancy's safe return.

"Nancy! We were so worried about you!" George cried out as she and Bess ran over to her.

"We didn't know what had happened," Bess said.

"I'm not sure what happened either," Nancy said wryly as Bess and George helped her down the steps. They led her up to the lounge and into an armchair by the fireplace. With a sigh of relief, Nancy began unbuckling her ski boots.

Mark came running with a stack of blankets, which he wrapped around Nancy. "You've had quite an evening," he said anxiously. "Thank goodness Gus went out with the ski patrol. He seemed to know you were out there and needed help. Are you hurt?"

"My leg aches a bit," Nancy admitted, rubbing her left leg. "I had to jump off the chair lift."

"You got stuck on the lift?" Christi said as she handed a mug of hot soup to Nancy. "How could that happen? Mark and I thought we had a foolproof system. The last skier of the day tells the top attendant that it's time to close."

"Well, it didn't work today," Nancy said. "The attendant told me to tell the guy at the top I was the last. But before I got there, the lift stopped."

"I promise you, Nancy," Christi said, "first thing tomorrow, we'll speak to the attendants. We'll figure out what happened."

Getting into bed that night, Nancy, Bess, and George went over the incident again. "I think it was more than just a case of mixed messages from the lift attendants," Nancy said. "Someone *planned* for me to get stuck on the lift."

"But who?" Bess asked. "And why?"

"We may be getting close to the truth," Nancy said, arranging a pillow under her sore leg. "Maybe someone wants to scare me off."

"What about Dexter Egan?" George said. "He has access to all the lift machinery."

"That's true, George," Nancy said. "Professor Hotchkiss or even Jacques could have paid Dexter to do it."

"Not Jacques!" Bess declared, putting down her hairbrush. "Nancy, Jacques would never do a thing like that!"

"Neither would Mark and Christi," George declared. "Or Lisa Ostrum or Meg or her mom—"

"And yet it has to be someone who's a guest or staff member here," Nancy finished. "That is, if we think it's the same person who vandalized the library. The fact is, we can't rule anyone out, at least not yet."

The girls snapped off the lights and nestled down in their beds. Exhausted, Nancy soon fell asleep. But her dreams played a garbled, disturbing stream of images—skis, chairlifts, dazzling gold rooms, hidden letters, the ransacked library . . .

Suddenly Nancy opened her eyes. She heard a slight noise near the door.

Nancy strained to peer across the dark room. She heard the sound again—a tiny swishing sound coming from beside her dresser.

Someone had sneaked into the room. She was sure of it!

14

The Discovery

"What do you think you're doing!" Nancy shouted as she sprang out of bed.

The figure in the shadows wheeled and leaped for the nearby door. Nancy started after the intruder, but her left leg was cramped and stiff. As she paused to straighten it, the door cracked open, and the person slid out into the hall. Nancy caught only a glimpse of a dark-hooded sweat-shirt on a crouched, furtive figure.

Still limping, Nancy grabbed her penlight from her jeans pocket. She headed to the door, which still stood ajar, and stepped into the hall. In the soft light of the wall lamps, she peered up and down the hall. No one was in sight.

Nancy hurried down to the nearest side corri-dor, the one leading to the back elevator. She snapped on her penlight and shone it down the dark corridor, but she saw no one. Frustrated, she returned to the main hallway. Whoever had been in her room must have gotten well away by now.

When she went back in her room, a bedside lamp had been turned on. George and Bess were sitting up in bed, looking anxiously toward the door.

"What happened?" George asked as Nancy came in, carefully closing and locking the door behind her.

"Somebody was in here snooping around in the dark," Nancy said. "I followed the person into the hall, but whoever it was had disappeared by the time I got there."

Switching on the lamp by her dresser, she carefully studied the items on top. "Comb, brush, lipgloss, sunscreen, ponytail clip . . . ," she said, checking each item against her memory.

"What do you think this person was looking for?" Bess asked.

"I have no idea," Nancy said, frowning. "I don't notice anything missing, but I have a feeling I may be overlooking something." She sighed as she turned off the lamp and went back to her bed. "I just can't put my finger on what it is."

At breakfast Friday morning, Mark Lane stopped by the small table where Nancy, Bess, and George had just finished eating. "The ski patrol is going to retrieve your skis and poles, and

I talked to both lift attendants," he told Nancy. "Bob, the man at the back lift, remembers telling you to carry the closing message to Pete, up at the top."

"And what did Pete say?" Nancy asked.

"Pete remembers some skier relaying that message," Mark said, "but he didn't pay any attention to who it was. He doesn't even remember if it was a man or a woman. With all the scarves and face protectors that skiers use, it's often hard to tell."

"I'll try to talk to Pete myself later on," Nancy said. "Thanks for the information, Mark."

"Somebody planned this," Nancy said as she and the cousins got up and left the dining room. "Someone got on the lift ahead of me, saw me get on, and went up and told Pete that he—or she— was the last skier of the day."

"So then Pete closed the lift and left you stranded all alone there in the cold," Bess said.

"That's right," Nancy said. "Pete had no way of knowing I was still on the lift. It was getting dark, and I was still halfway down the mountain."

"What a rotten thing for someone to do," George said as they turned down the hall to the lobby. "But how do we know if it's the same person who vandalized the library?"

Nancy shook her head. "My intuition tells me all these things are connected," she said. "Somebody was looking for something in the library, either in the wall or in the books—" She came to a sudden halt. "Wait a minute! That's it!"

"What's 'it,' Nan?" Bess asked.

"I think I know what our visitor last night was after!" Nancy called over her shoulder as she dashed off, heading for the main stairs.

The three girls ran up the two flights of stairs to the third floor. Nancy charged into their room and stood squarely in front of the dresser. "Just as I thought," she announced triumphantly. "That old red book I borrowed from the library—it's gone!"

"The one about Marie Antoinette?" Bess asked.

"Right!" Nancy said. "I had it with me down in the lounge last night after dinner. I remember laying it down here when I came back up. Whoever came prowling last night took that book."

"But why would anyone want it that badly?" George asked.

"If it came from Chateau Rochemont, it may hold a clue about where Marie Antoinette's letters were hidden," Nancy said. "Which means that somebody else may find the letters before Jacques does!" She grabbed her penlight and lock-picking kit. "Come on, guys, we don't have a minute to waste. Let's get to the tower room."

A few minutes later, the girls were making their way down the long basement corridor. Even in the daytime, the windowless hallway was dark and forbidding. Nancy flashed her penlight straight ahead until they saw the door to the tower stairs.

Nancy picked open the lock, and the girls stepped inside the room with the embossed wooden feathers. Nancy found the protruding feather and gave it a tug. The panel at the end wall slid up.

Nancy stepped through the panel and into the small room at the bottom of the circular stairs. "Okay, guys," she started to say, "let's—" She stopped in midsentence, staring at the opposite wall. "Hang on," she said. "What's that on the outside wall?"

The girls studied the wall across from the door. Daylight shone in through the thinnest possible crack, cutting a tall rectangle in the stone outer wall.

"It looks like a door!" Bess whispered in amazement.

"That must be the door that the snowmobiler in black was looking for on Tuesday," Nancy said. "I knew I saw that person tugging on something on the tower wall."

"We couldn't see it when we were here the other night," Bess said. "But with the sunlight shining through now, it's visible."

"And look here!" Nancy flashed her light up and down the edges. "The door has been opened recently—all these old cobwebs are broken."

"Maybe the snowmobiler finally found the other entrance," George said.

"Someone did," Nancy said. "Let's see if we can get the door open." She examined the area for a door handle but found none. "Maybe it swings outward. Let's try giving it a hard push."

Together the girls threw their weight against the door, but it didn't budge.

"You know what?" Nancy said, suddenly dropping her voice to a whisper. "If someone did get in this way, whoever it is might still be up there. Come on, guys. We'd better go see what's going on."

The girls started up the rickety stairs, careful to avoid the broken step where George had fallen through. At the top, Nancy pushed open the door to the small narrow hall and stepped in. George and Bess followed close behind.

Nancy tiptoed across the landing and pressed her ear against the door. She listened intently for a moment, then shook her head. "I don't hear anybody," she whispered to her friends. "Let's try the door."

Nancy turned the knob and eased the door open. The round room beyond was dark.

Cautiously, Nancy flashed her light into the room. "Nobody's here," she said in relief. "Let's go on in." She reached around and snapped on the light switch. The crystal chandelier blazed with light.

"That is the most beautiful thing," Bess said, staring up at the elaborate glass fixture. "Look at all those delicate crystal flowers holding up the lightbulbs and all those gorgeous crystal pendants. When all the dust has been cleaned off, I bet it'll sparkle just like a mass of diamonds."

"Yeah, but what a job—cleaning all those gorgeous crystal pendants," George said with a wry smile. "And imagine what it was like in the days when it was lit by candles instead of lightbulbs. How would you like to scrape candle drippings off all those pendants?"

Nancy glanced around the room. Beside the gold embossed wall, spread out on the floor, were Jacques's tools. Next to them was his footstool with a folded sweatshirt lying on top.

Curiously, Nancy walked across the round room. Something was amiss. She wasn't sure just what it was, but something about the room didn't feel right.

She knelt down and picked up the sweatshirt. Three gilded leaves lay underneath the stool.

That's odd, she thought, glancing around. Where did these gold leaves come from? Jacques had said that he always replaced each leaf he removed, fitting it back into its special spot on the wall.

And then she saw it. Just a few inches above the floor, there was a small hole in the wall panel. Quickly, Nancy knelt down and flashed her light into the opening. Inside was a neatly finished square cavity.

Was this the niche Jacques's great-grandfather had told him about? she wondered. The niche that held the queen's letters? Holding her breath, Nancy shoved her hand inside.

The niche was empty.

15

A Vital Clue

Nancy turned to face George and Bess. "We've got to get back downstairs!" she said urgently. "Someone has already found the queen's letters."

"You're kidding!" George said in disbelief.

"It has to be whoever broke into our room and took that book," Nancy said, striding swiftly toward the stairs. "If we can just find who has the red book now, I bet we'll find the letters, too."

Bess and George trotted after her. "But how do we find the red book?" George asked.

"We search everybody's rooms," Nancy called over her shoulder as she reached the winding staircase. "This is a perfect time—just about all the guests will be out on the ski slopes this morning. Let's go ask Mark and Christi for a passkey."

The three girls hurried down the stairs and

soon emerged in the basement corridor. A few minutes later, they were upstairs knocking on the Lanes' office door.

Mark and Christi were surprised when Nancy told them about the nighttime intruder, the missing book, and the empty cavity in the tower room wall. But they readily handed Nancy a key that would open all the guest room doors.

"I was just thinking," Mark said while Christi was photocopying for the girls a list of the guests' room numbers. "The red book is written in French, right? So aren't we looking for someone who can read French? That makes Jacques look pretty suspicious."

"That's true," Nancy said. "But why would he steal the red book from me? I would have given it to him if he'd asked. No, I think we have to find someone else who reads French. We know Professor Hotchkiss does, so we'll search his room first. But other guests may know French, too. We'll just have to keep looking until the book turns up."

"I haven't found anything here at all," George said in Professor Hotchkiss's room a short time later. "Have you, Nancy?"

"Not a thing," Nancy said, looking around.

"Maybe he took the red book with him," Bess suggested.

"Out on the slopes?" George asked skeptically.

"Okay, maybe not," Bess said. "Whose room do we search next, Nancy?"

"We'll move down the hall in order," Nancy said. "It'll be faster that way."

"So who's next door to Professor Hotchkiss?" George asked as they left his room.

Nancy studied the guest list that Christi had provided them. "Lisa Ostrum," she said.

"Well, that shouldn't take long," George said as the girls headed toward her door. "I doubt that Lisa's behind any of this. After all, she got trapped in the fake stairway. She's a victim, not a culprit."

"True, but I overheard Lisa and the professor talking about Marie Antoinette at breakfast the other morning," Nancy said, fitting the passkey into Lisa's door. "That shows Lisa has some interest in the subject."

The girls stepped inside Lisa's room. "Bess, you start with the desk over there," Nancy said. "And, George, you can—" She stopped in mid-sentence, staring in the direction of the bed.

A small table, covered with magazines and newspapers, sat next to Lisa's bed. Right under the top magazine, a corner of a small book poked out.

"The red book!" George exclaimed.

"Does that mean Lisa was the person in our room last night?" Bess asked.

"It sure looks that way, Bess," Nancy said, picking up the book. "She must have figured that

134

the red book held a clue to whatever was in the tower."

"But how did she know that we had the book in our room?" George asked.

"I had it with me in the lounge last night," Nancy recalled. "When I came up, I passed Lisa on the stairs. She must have noticed the book then. If she'd already searched the library, looking for clues, she would have known what that book was."

"But the night we discovered the library had been vandalized, Lisa said she could only read Spanish, not French," George remembered.

"She probably said that just to throw people off her track," Nancy said.

"I wonder if Lisa was the person out by the tower in the black snowmobile suit," Bess said.

"She may have been, Bess," Nancy agreed. "And if she took the red book, then I'll bet she's the one who beat Jacques to the queen's letters. Come on, guys, let's get busy. Let's search this room!"

Nancy assigned each girl a section, and they set to work hunting for the letters.

"Hey, what do we have here!" Bess said a short time later as she picked up Lisa's camera bag. "This side pocket feels pretty bulky to me." She unsnapped the pocket and reached inside.

"What is it, Bess?" Nancy asked.

Bess carefully pulled out a tiny bundle of folded thin papers, all held together with a

135

frayed pink ribbon. "The queen's letters?" she asked in a hushed voice.

"They look exactly like the bundle of letters Jacques described," Nancy said, awestruck. "Quick, let's straighten up so Lisa won't know we were here. Then we can take the letters back to our room and check them out."

Once the girls were back in their room, Nancy carefully untied the pink ribbon and took one of the letters off the top. "The writing is faded, and the paper's really old and brittle," Nancy said. "But this letter sure is written in French."

"She must have used a quill pen," George remarked, looking at another letter. "The writing is awfully scratchy."

"Hey!" Bess said, frowning as she studied a letter. "This one is signed by somebody else." She squinted at the signature. "It's not Marie Antoinette. It looks more like . . . Rochelle?" she said finally. "Does that make any sense?"

Nancy looked at the signature on the letter she had opened. "This one's signed by someone named Rochelle, too."

"Same here," George said, looking at the letter in her hand. "Signed by Rochelle. I wonder who *she* was."

"Well, whoever she was," Bess said, clearly disappointed, "she wasn't the queen."

"No," Nancy agreed. "But her letters may still be important. Maybe I can translate some of this."

Carefully, Nancy began reading the top letter. "It starts with some trip Rochelle made from Paris," she translated. "Rochelle seems to work for someone, someone she considers very important."

"Like maybe the queen?" Bess asked.

"You read my thoughts, Bess," Nancy said. "She may have been a servant of the queen." Nancy paused for a moment as she studied the letter.

"Hey, here's something!" she said. "'*Le plus grand diamant de ma reine,*'" she read out loud. "'My queen's largest diamond,'" she translated.

"Now we're getting somewhere!" George said excitedly. "What else does it say, Nancy?"

"'*Ma reine a caché le diamant dans le lustre de la chambre d'or, parce qu'elle avait peur des révolutionnaires,*'" Nancy went on. "Let's see. That sounds like: 'My queen has hidden the diamond in the chandelier of the gold room because she is afraid of the revolutionaries.'"

"But how could she hide it in the chandelier?" Bess asked.

Nancy snapped her fingers. "Of course! Remember all those tiny crystal pendants hanging from the chandelier?"

"Sure," Bess said. "They are so cool."

"What if one of them is more than just a piece of crystal?" Nancy asked.

"You mean like maybe one of them is a diamond?" George asked.

137

"You got it, George," Nancy said. "According to Rochelle's letter, when the French Revolution started, the queen was afraid that the rebels would find her biggest diamond. So she hid it. And what better place to hide a diamond pendant than dangling right in plain sight, surrounded by a hundred others that look exactly like it."

"So the diamond pendant could still be up there in the tower room," Bess said. "Wow!"

"Possibly," Nancy said, placing the letter on top of the pile. "I'll bet Lisa has read this and figured out where the diamond was hidden. We'd better get back up to the tower room now—before it's too late."

"Let's go!" George said, jumping to her feet.

"On second thought," Nancy said, rising hesitantly, "maybe you guys should wait in the basement locker room. If Lisa comes in from the slopes, you could stall her somehow. I don't want her to find me searching for the diamond."

The girls ran down the large front stairs, passing the main lounge as they headed toward the lower level. As they did, Gus jumped up from in front of the fire, giving an enthusiastic bark.

"Not now, boy," Nancy said, holding up one hand. "We'll have time to play later. I promise."

They hurried on down the stairs to the basement, where George and Bess stationed themselves near their lockers. Nancy sprinted on down the corridor that led to the circular staircase.

A few moments later, Nancy reached the door of the secret round room. She thrust it open and stepped inside.

The crystal chandelier was blazing brightly. In the middle of the room, directly under the chandelier, stood Jacques's stepladder.

And high on the ladder, standing next to the crystal chandelier, was Lisa Ostrum. In her left hand she held a sparkling pendant!

Lisa turned and glared furiously down at Nancy. "You!" she spat out angrily. "Snooping again, Nancy Drew? Well, this time you're going to be very sorry!"

Then, like a shot, Lisa sprang from the ladder and lunged at Nancy.

16

Rescue!

As Lisa Ostrum lunged at Nancy, Nancy quickly turned sideways and raised her foot, preparing for a karate kick. "Better watch it, Lisa!" she warned.

Lisa still advanced. Nancy shot her right leg out, but Lisa twisted quickly away. "You may think you're the only one who knows karate, Nancy," Lisa sneered. "But, trust me, you're not!" She crouched expertly in a karate stance.

She's not kidding, Nancy thought. Slowly she began circling Lisa. With her gaze fixed on Nancy's face, Lisa also moved around in a slow circle. Nancy stayed silent, concentrating on Lisa's every move.

Suddenly Lisa moved forward, letting out a loud karate yell. The hard side of her right hand flew toward Nancy's throat.

Nancy jumped back, barely avoiding the blow.

"You'll never get away with this, Lisa," Nancy said.

"Of course I will," Lisa said angrily. "The only person standing between that diamond and me is you. And you won't be standing there much longer. After all I've gone through, do you think I'm going to give up now?"

"And what exactly have you 'gone through,'" Lisa?" Nancy asked, stalling for time, eyes glued on her opponent.

"Finding this room, for one thing!" Lisa replied. "I thought I'd never find that outer entrance to the tower, those stupid winding stairs, and that hidden entrance. And I had to go through all the books in the library in the first place, trying to figure out what treasure was hidden in the tower. It was pure luck that I found that note inside the red book."

"What note?" Nancy asked.

Lisa let out a contemptuous laugh. "A note written by Rochelle de Chaffin, tucked inside that red book," she said. "I had to put it back in the library so no one would find it on me. It said she had hidden her letters in the panel of the tower wall."

"Then why did you vandalize that beautiful library?"

Lisa's eyes narrowed. "My French is only rudimentary, and I thought the note said the library wall. So I gouged out the wall behind the painting and couldn't find a niche. Then I remem-

141

bered Mark saying that the library paneling came from England, not France. I realized Rochelle meant the wall inside the tower. So I found it— no thanks to you and your nosy friends."

"So that was you in the black snowmobile suit on Tuesday, looking for a doorway outside the tower," Nancy said.

"Yeah," Lisa said nastily. "By the way, how does your leg feel?" She made a sudden move, trying to catch Nancy off guard. Nancy deftly sidestepped the attack.

"As you can see, my leg's fine now," Nancy answered. "How about that stalled elevator Sunday night—you again?"

"You bet," Lisa said. "I was down exploring the lower level when I heard you and George talking about how you're a detective. I knew you were after my treasure. When I heard you go into that elevator, it was just too tempting. I flipped the switch to trap you inside."

"Didn't you learn then that we don't scare easily?" Nancy said. A split second later, she made a quick jab at Lisa with her foot. Lisa parried it neatly, almost knocking Nancy off balance.

"I figured I'd beat you to the treasure anyway," Lisa said. "But then, last night after dinner, I saw you carrying that red book. I didn't want you to figure out where the letters were, so I took it from your room."

"Lisa," Nancy said, taking a tiny step forward, "why is this diamond so important to you?"

"Why!" Lisa said angrily. "Because it's worth hundreds of thousands of dollars. Obviously, you have no idea how little I'm paid for my articles. You can't imagine what I go through, trying to live on my tiny income. This diamond will bring me enough money to do anything I like." She paused, watching Nancy. "But enough talk!" she said, suddenly lunging forward and striking at Nancy's throat.

Nancy jumped away, but the blow landed on her shoulder. Nancy countered with a loud karate yell and a hard chop to Lisa's arm.

Just then the door swung open. Gus, the sheepdog, came charging in, heading directly for Lisa.

"Stop it, you filthy animal!" Lisa screamed.

Gus jumped high in the air, coming down with his front paws hard on Lisa's shoulders. Lisa fell to the floor, and Gus pinned her there, growling, his teeth just a few inches from her throat.

George and Bess burst into the room. "Nancy, are you okay?" George asked, out of breath.

"I'm fine, now," Nancy said. "But a few minutes ago, I wasn't so sure. Thank heavens you guys got here when you did."

"You can thank Gus for that," Bess said. "He came charging through the locker room like a big furry tornado, heading for the long corridor. He looked like he knew where he was going, so we followed him."

Nancy grabbed some rope out of Jacques's toolbox and knelt down next to Lisa. "Okay, boy," she said to Gus. "We'll tie Lisa's hands behind her back, and then you can let her go."

A moment later Gus backed off as the three girls pulled Lisa to her feet. "Lisa," Nancy said, "we're going to get you down that staircase and back to Mark and Christi's office. And after that, you just may have a little visit from the local police."

"This is such an intriguing story," Professor Hotchkiss said that evening as Wickford Castle's guests gathered around a roaring fire in the lounge.

"It certainly is," Dr. Alvarez said. "Nancy, how did Lisa know there was a treasure in the tower?"

"On Lisa's first visit to the castle," Nancy said, "Mark must have told the guests his story about Marie Antoinette hiding something of value in the tower room."

"I always say that," Mark said with a chuckle. "But I never thought it was really true."

"Well, Lisa thought it was true," Nancy said. "So she decided to return and hunt for the treasure. She couldn't get into the tower, so she started looking for clues, beginning with the library. She tore it apart, searching for clues about the tower. She was your library vandal, Mark."

From the back of the room, Dexter Egan spoke up. "I wondered who did that," he said. "Monday morning, after Mark told me you folks had found this big mess in the library the night before, I got curious. So that afternoon, I left work and went up to the library. I used my own key to get in. I looked in a whole lot of books, and I searched in that hole in the wall. But I sure couldn't make sense out of it."

"So that was why you were hiding in the library the day Bess, George, and I came in there," Nancy said.

Dexter's eyebrows shot up. "You knew I was there?" he said. "I thought I hid real good. I was supposed to be out working, you see. I didn't want to get in trouble with Mark and Christi."

Mark smiled good-naturedly. "Don't worry about it, Dexter."

"So how did *you* guys learn where the treasure was?" Meg asked Nancy.

"Tuesday night," Nancy explained, "George, Bess, and I discovered the stairs to the tower room. We went up and found Jacques searching for the letters his great-grandfather had told him about."

"The girls persuaded me to tell Mark and Christi of my search," Jacques added.

"Yes," Nancy said, "but while we were in the office, I saw someone in the hall, listening in. It must have been Lisa. That's how she learned that Jacques was searching for the letters, too."

"So was it Lisa who hit me during the skating party?" Meg asked. "Mistaking me for Jacques?"

"It sure was, Meg," Nancy said. "She followed you and Jacques to the end of the pond. In the darkness, when she saw Jacques's purple cap, she went for it with a rock. She wanted to put Jacques out of commission, so he wouldn't find the letters first."

"Sorry, Meg," Jacques said, shaking his head.

"It wasn't your fault, Jacques," Meg replied, smiling sweetly at Jacques. Nearby, Nancy heard Bess sigh and saw her roll her eyes.

"Nancy, what about when Lisa got trapped on the fake stairs?" Christi asked. "Surely she didn't do that to herself."

"Yes, she did—to take suspicion off herself," Nancy said. "When Lisa saw the skeleton key in the door, she must have taken it out, stepped in, and locked the door from the inside. Then she put the key in her pocket and started calling for help. The next day, out by the snowmobiles, we saw someone in a black snowmobile suit drop the key in the snow. We now know it was Lisa."

"And Lisa was responsible for stranding Nancy on the chairlift," Christi said. "When we showed Lisa's ski parka to Pete, he said she must have been the person who told him that she was the last skier of the day. She knew he would close down the lift, leaving Nancy hanging there in the cold."

"But Lisa couldn't have been the one who sawed through that step on the circular staircase Tuesday night," Bess said. "You know, the one that George fell through?"

"That's right," George piped up. "Lisa hadn't found her way into the tower yet on Tuesday."

Dexter Egan cleared his throat uneasily. "It was me," he spoke up. "I've already told Mark and Christi everything. Now I'll tell you. Mark started asking me all these questions about my past, and I figured you put him up to it, Ms. Drew. So I sawed the step to scare you girls away. I didn't want anyone to know I'd done time in prison. I thought I might lose my job."

"We've decided to give Dexter a second chance," Christi said.

"I swear I never wanted to hurt anybody," Dexter went on. "I sure didn't think anyone would fall clear through that step. I just wanted to stop you from investigating any more." He looked at Nancy. "I'm sorry."

"Well, I must say, Lisa Ostrum is a clever young woman," Professor Hotchkiss said. "I must admit, I was looking for a way into the tower, too. But I don't suppose I ever would have found it."

The guests turned to look at the white-haired professor in surprise.

"I didn't travel all the way from northern

147

Massachusetts to Wisconsin just to ski," the professor went on. "As most of you know, I have a long-standing interest in Marie Antoinette. During my research, I read about Rochelle de Chaffin, one of the queen's ladies-in-waiting. She survived the French Revolution, and in her old age, she hinted that the queen had left a treasure hidden somewhere. Later I learned that the tower of Chateau Rochemont had been transplanted to Wisconsin. Knowing of Marie Antoinette's love for the chateau, I began to wonder if the tower held her secret. A wild hunch, perhaps, but I thought it worth a trip. I pretended to be on a ski vacation, though. I didn't want other scholars to guess what I was up to."

"You *were* on our suspect list for a while, Professor," George admitted. "That day when you came in the locker room wearing that black snowmobile outfit, we were really suspicious."

"Sheer coincidence," the professor declared. "I had been out earlier on one of the guest snowmobiles. But now I know why you young ladies looked at me so strangely when I came in. It unnerved me, I must say."

"I guess that clears everything up," Mark said. "Thanks to Nancy Drew, the hidden letters have been found and a priceless diamond has been discovered. And Lisa Ostrum is safely in jail where she belongs."

"The only question left now," Christi said, "is

deciding what we should do with all these valuable items. Mark and I have talked it over, and we'd like to return the diamond to the French government. After all, it came here from France."

"A fine idea," Professor Hotchkiss said.

"But Rochelle's letters are something else," Mark said. "We realize how much the letters meant to Jacques and how hard he searched for them."

"But, Mark," Jacques said, "my search was for the memory of my great-grandfather. I have no personal desire to own the letters."

"I have a suggestion," Dr. Alvarez said. "Why not return the letters along with the diamond to the French government? You could make it a special gift in memory of Jacques's great-grandfather."

"That's a great idea," Christi said.

"Nothing would please me more," Jacques said. "But we must ask France to let the professor study and publish the letters first. I appreciate his love for my country's history. I know he would do a fine job in translating and understanding these letters."

"Jacques," Professor Hotchkiss said warmly, "I would be pleased and proud to have that opportunity. Thank you so much."

"And thank you, Nancy," Christi said, "for all you've done for Wickford Castle and Butter Ridge Winter Sports Area. We won't be bothered by mysterious night noises anymore, and the publicity surrounding this historical discovery should be bringing lots of attention to our resort."

"Look who else has come to say thank you to Nancy," Mark said, nodding toward the door.

Gus came happily trotting into the lounge and sat down beside Nancy.

"I'm the one who should thank Gus," Nancy said as she leaned down and stroked his shaggy coat. "After all, Gus helped the ski patroller find me the night I got stranded on the lift. And it was Gus who pinned down Lisa in the tower room."

As Nancy leaned down to give him a big hug, Gus jumped up. Tail wagging, he gave Nancy's face a couple of big, sloppy licks.

Nancy giggled and laid her cheek against his head. "You'd make a great detective yourself, Gus," she declared. "We'll have to team up again some day!"

THE HARDY BOYS® SERIES By Franklin W. Dixon

NANCY DREW® MYSTERY STORIES By Carolyn Keene

- [ ] #58: THE FLYING SAUCER MYSTERY — 72320-0/$3.99
- [ ] #62: THE KACHINA DOLL MYSTERY — 67220-7/$3.99
- [ ] #68: THE ELUSIVE HEIRESS — 62478-4/$3.99
- [ ] #72: THE HAUNTED CAROUSEL — 66227-9/$3.99
- [ ] #73: ENEMY MATCH — 64283-9/$3.50
- [ ] #77: THE BLUEBEARD ROOM — 66857-9/$3.50
- [ ] #78: THE PHANTOM OF VENICE — 73422-9/$3.50
- [ ] #79: THE DOUBLE HORROR OF FENLEY PLACE — 64387-8/$3.99
- [ ] #81: MARDI GRAS MYSTERY — 64961-2/$3.99
- [ ] #83: THE CASE OF THE VANISHING VEIL — 63413-5/$3.99
- [ ] #84: THE JOKER'S REVENGE — 63414-3/$3.99
- [ ] #85: THE SECRET OF SHADY GLEN — 63416-X/$3.99
- [ ] #87: THE CASE OF THE RISING STAR — 66312-7/$3.99
- [ ] #89: THE CASE OF THE DISAPPEARING DEEJAY — 66314-3/$3.99
- [ ] #91: THE GIRL WHO COULDN'T REMEMBER — 66316-X/$3.99
- [ ] #92: THE GHOST OF CRAVEN COVE — 66317-8/$3.99
- [ ] #93: THE CASE OF THE SAFECRACKER'S SECRET — 66318-6/$3.99
- [ ] #94: THE PICTURE-PERFECT MYSTERY — 66319-4/$3.99
- [ ] #96: THE CASE OF THE PHOTO FINISH — 69281-X/$3.99
- [ ] #97: THE MYSTERY AT MAGNOLIA MANSION — 69282-8/$3.99
- [ ] #98: THE HAUNTING OF HORSE ISAND — 69284-4/$3.99
- [ ] #99: THE SECRET AT SEVEN ROCKS — 69285-2/$3.99
- [ ] #101: THE MYSTERY OF THE MISSING MILLIONAIRES — 69287-9/$3.99
- [ ] #102: THE SECRET IN THE DARK — 69279-8/$3.99
- [ ] #103: THE STRANGER IN THE SHADOWS — 73049-5/$3.99
- [ ] #104: THE MYSTERY OF THE JADE TIGER — 73050-9/$3.99
- [ ] #105: THE CLUE IN THE ANTIQUE TRUNK — 73051-7/$3.99
- [ ] #107: THE LEGEND OF MINER'S CREEK — 73053-3/$3.99

- [ ] #109: THE MYSTERY OF THE MASKED RIDER — 73055-X/$3.99
- [ ] #110: THE NUTCRACKER BALLET MYSTERY — 73056-8/$3.99
- [ ] #111: THE SECRET AT SOLAIRE — 79297-0/$3.99
- [ ] #112: CRIME IN THE QUEEN'S COURT — 79298-9/$3.99
- [ ] #113: THE SECRET LOST AT SEA — 79299-7/$3.99
- [ ] #114: THE SEARCH FOR THE SILVER PERSIAN — 79300-4/$3.99
- [ ] #115: THE SUSPECT IN THE SMOKE — 79301-2/$3.99
- [ ] #116: THE CASE OF THE TWIN TEDDY BEARS — 79302-0/$3.99
- [ ] #117: MYSTERY ON THE MENU — 79303-9/$3.99
- [ ] #118: TROUBLE AT LAKE TAHOE — 79304-7/$3.99
- [ ] #119: THE MYSTERY OF THE MISSING MASCOT — 87202-8/$3.99
- [ ] #120: THE CASE OF THE FLOATING CRIME — 87203-6/$3.99
- [ ] #121: THE FORTUNE-TELLER'S SECRET — 87204-4/$3.99
- [ ] #122: THE MESSAGE IN THE HAUNTED MANSION — 87205-2/$3.99
- [ ] #123: THE CLUE ON THE SILVER SCREEN — 87206-0/$3.99
- [ ] #124: THE SECRET OF THE SCARLET HAND — 87207-9/$3.99
- [ ] #125: THE TEEN MODEL MYSTERY — 87208-7/$3.99
- [ ] #126: THE RIDDLE IN THE RARE BOOK — 87209-5/$3.99
- [ ] #127: THE CASE OF THE DANGEROUS SOLUTION — 50500-9/$3.99
- [ ] #128: THE TREASURE IN THE ROYAL TOWER — 50502-5/$3.99
- [ ] NANCY DREW GHOST STORIES - #1 — 69132-5/$3.99

A MINSTREL® BOOK

Published by Pocket Books